The Demolition Mission

The zebra-striped car Rusk was driving caught up with Joe's Purple Machine. Rusk accelerated to full speed and smashed into the back of Joe's junker.

Joe felt the breath forced out of him. Without the shoulder harness, he would have flown through the windshield. Clearing his head, Joe realized his engine had stalled. He turned the key and pumped the gas pedal.

Wham! The zebra-striped car hit again, knocking the Purple Machine sideways. Joe turned the key once more, but the engine didn't even grind.

Joe decided he had better get out of the junker. Struggling with the harness, he heard Rusk's roaring car heading straight for him.

Frank sprinted out into the arena toward the Purple Machine. As he ran, the black-and-white car crashed broadside into Joe's car.

"Joe!" Frank cried. But Joe had vanished, buried in the grinding metal of the now crushed Purple Machine.

The Hardy Boys Mystery Stories

Available from MINSTREL Books

112

The HARDY BOYS®

THE DEMOLITION MISSION

FRANKLIN W. DIXON

A MINSTREL® BOOK

PUBLISHED BY POCKET BOOKS

New York   London   Toronto   Sydney   Tokyo   Singapore

This book is a work of fiction. Names, characters, places, and incidents are either the product of the author's imagination or are used fictitiously. Any resemblance to actual events or locales or persons, living or dead, is entirely coincidental.

A MINSTREL PAPERBACK *ORIGINAL*

A Minstrel Book published by
POCKET BOOKS, a division of Simon & Schuster Inc.
1230 Avenue of the Americas, New York, NY 10020

Copyright © 1992 by Simon & Schuster Inc.
Cover artwork copyright © 1992 by Paul Bachem
Produced by Mega-Books of New York, Inc.

ISBN: 0-671-73058-4

First Minstrel Books printing February 1992

10 9 8 7 6 5 4 3 2

THE HARDY BOYS MYSTERY STORIES is a trademark of Simon & Schuster Inc.

THE HARDY BOYS, A MINSTREL BOOK and colophon are registered trademarks of Simon & Schuster Inc.

Printed in the U.S.A.

Contents

THE DEMOLITION
MISSION

1 Out of Control

"Joe!" Frank Hardy shouted to his brother from the front stoop of the Hardys' house. "Look out for that jeep!"

Blond-haired Joe Hardy's head snapped back quickly from under the open hood of the brothers' blue van. As he jumped to safety on the curb, he caught sight of the driver of the jeep that was barreling his way. It was the Hardys' friend Chet Morton.

"I can't stop in time!" Chet cried out from behind the wheel of the beat-up old jeep. The younger Hardy saw that the jeep was green and rusty, with more rust on it than paint. Joe also knew that if Chet didn't swerve out of the way within the

1

next few seconds, his jeep was going to plow into the front of the van.

"It's the brakes!" Chet called out frantically. "They need adjusting!"

"Downshift, then kill the engine!" Joe shouted.

He and Frank watched as Chet turned the wheel to avoid hitting the van. He fumbled with the stick shift, and the jeep lurched and slowed down. Chet switched off the engine and swung the jeep into the Hardys' driveway, where it rocked and jolted to a stop inches from the garage door.

"This is the new car you were raving about?" Frank asked, stepping across the lawn to the driveway.

"Okay, so it needs a little work," Chet said with a shrug as he climbed out of the frayed driver's seat. Chet was large-boned and had curly brown hair.

"I'd say this thing needed a little work ten years ago," Joe said.

"It's a collector's item," Chet insisted. "The guy at Major Motors told me this was one of the first civilian jeeps made. He said when the company started up the assembly line, they built a few prototypes to see if everything was working right. This was a test car. It wasn't even for sale."

"If it wasn't for sale," Joe asked his friend, "how did you buy it?"

"Through some pretty shrewd dealing," Chet said with a proud smile.

"Well, it makes sense to drive one prototype over to the speedway to see another prototype," Frank said. "But," he added, running his fingers through his dark brown hair, "when you insisted on driving us there, we assumed your car had brakes."

"The linkage just needs a little oil, that's all," Chet said defensively.

"And maybe a couple of brake drums," Joe added.

Chet ignored Joe's remark. "So tell me about this new sports car we're going to see," he said.

"Dad set it up for us," Frank told Chet. "He got a call this morning from Felix Stock out at Bayport Motor Speedway."

"Stock's that hotshot engineer who thinks he can take on the big automakers," Joe added. "He was written up in the *Examiner*."

"I read that article," Chet said. "It said Stock's put every dime he has into developing a high-performance sports car he's named the Orion or something."

"It's called the Saurion," Frank said. "It's a two-seater designed to compete with sports cars like the Corvette and Lotus."

"Stock thought Frank and I would like to take it for a spin," Joe added, grinning.

"Actually, Stock wants us to check on a couple of strange incidents that have taken place out at the speedway," Frank said. "Stock thinks someone

3

might be trying to sabotage the development of his new car. And since Dad's busy working on a case for the U.S. Treasury Department," Frank continued, "he asked us to handle this investigation."

Frank and Joe's father, Fenton Hardy, a former New York City police officer, had become a well-known private detective who worked on federal as well as individual and police cases.

The Hardy brothers had used what their father had taught them about detective work to crack their own cases. Although Frank was only eighteen and his brother was a year younger, they had investigated countless crimes in Bayport and all over the world.

"We'd better get out to the track," Joe urged them. He jogged over to the van and slammed the hood shut. Joe had been trying to diagnose the cause of a troubling clicking noise coming from under the hood. He removed a small plastic tube of silicone from the van's tool chest, then locked the doors. "Feed that heap of yours some of this," he told Chet.

"Why is Stock building his car out at the speedway?" Chet asked, taking the tube of silicone from Joe. "Doesn't he have his own garage?"

"Stock made some kind of a deal with Curt Kiser," Frank explained while Chet applied the silicone to the jeep's brake cable. "Kiser owns the speedway."

4

"Stock's only got a couple of days left to make sure the Saurion's ready," Joe added. "It's scheduled to race that new Japanese company's sports car Saturday night."

"The Sata Speedster," Chet said. "I read about that car, too. It's supposed to be incredibly fast."

"Dad said Felix Stock claims it won't even be a contest," Joe said.

"Is Stock *really* going to let you drive the Saurion?" Chet asked.

Frank nodded. "We had to promise Aunt Gertrude we'd be sure to follow the speed limit," he said, rolling his eyes.

"There isn't any speed limit on a racetrack," Chet reminded Frank.

"*We* know that," Joe said. "But we didn't want Aunt Gert to worry about us any more than she already does."

Just then a middle-aged woman appeared on the front porch of the Hardys' house. "You boys be careful, now," Aunt Gertrude called. "Make sure you wear helmets and safety belts and—"

"We will, Aunt Gertrude, don't worry," Frank said, pulling Joe and Chet over toward the jeep. The three friends piled into the jeep and waved at Aunt Gertrude. Then Chet backed the car down the driveway and headed toward Shore Road.

Twenty minutes later Joe glanced at his watch. "If we'd driven our van, we would have reached the speedway by now," he said. Chet's jeep had stalled twice, and from the way the old car occasionally vibrated, Joe concluded it had a loose tie-rod, broken engine mount, or maybe both. "Take a left at the next road," Joe told Chet, "if you can."

"Give me a break, will you?" Chet pleaded.

"Yeah, Joe," Frank said. "I can see the speedway gate right at the end of this road. It shouldn't take us more than a couple of hours to reach it."

As they pulled up to the speedway entrance, a uniformed guard in the booth stepped outside. "You here for the demolition derby?" he asked, staring at Chet's jeep.

"Very funny," Chet muttered. Joe chuckled.

Frank gave the guard their names. "We're here to see Mr. Stock," he said. "He's expecting us."

"You'll need grounds passes," the security guard told them. "They're issued from the speedway office. Just follow this road around to the left."

As they drove through the gate, Frank studied the sprawling speedway. The main gate was opposite the center of the huge, two-mile oval. Beyond the spectators' parking lot and the aluminum spectator stands to the right, Frank spotted several low garages in the infield. These housed the demolition derby operations. Stretching around the oval was Gasoline Alley, a group of garages for the race cars. Two of the buildings that stood behind and to the left of the viewing stand and starting line were

6

modern corrugated metal structures that gleamed in the midmorning sun. But Frank noticed that most of the garages around the oval were old and ramshackle. In fact, he thought the speedway generally looked run-down.

"There are the offices." Joe pointed at a one-story cement-block building. As they approached it, he could see that paint was peeling from the steel-frame windows. Chet parked in the small lot beside the office.

A tall, muscular man with mirrored sunglasses and black hair and mustache stepped out the front door and came up to the jeep. "You must be the Hardys," the man said, folding his arms at chest height. "I'm Curt Kiser, owner of the speedway."

Frank introduced Chet, then Joe and himself.

"I have your grounds passes right here." He handed out the tags. "Felix Stock told me to expect you," Kiser added. "I'll take you over to meet him. He's in Gasoline Alley."

Frank got the impression that Kiser was a man of no nonsense. Looking to his right, Frank saw a golf cart with the Bayport Motor Speedway logo painted on it zip up to the parking area.

"This is Jason Dain, my assistant," Kiser announced, pointing to the smiling cart driver. He introduced the Hardys and Chet to his assistant, who had long reddish blond hair.

If Kiser's greeting was abrupt, Joe thought that

Jason Dain treated them like old friends. "Hey, good to see you!" he said enthusiastically. "I'll meet you guys over there." Then he turned the cart and headed off in the direction of Gasoline Alley.

Curt Kiser signaled Chet and the others to follow him.

"I've been to this track before," Frank said as they walked past Kiser's office, "but this is my first visit to Gasoline Alley." When they reached the alley, Frank looked into the garages where the racing cars were prepared. In the newer garages mechanics were bending over brightly painted race cars, making the adjustments aimed at squeezing that last millisecond of speed out of the racers.

"There's the Saurion!" Joe said suddenly, pointing toward a sleek, deep red metallic automobile inside a garage. The sign above the overhead door read Stock Motor Car Company, and under that, Building A.

"Hey, Felix!" Curt Kiser called into the garage. "The Hardys are here."

A man hurried over to them from the shadowy interior of the building. Frank noticed that Felix Stock, who was in his thirties, was tanned and trim, with short brown hair. The press said Felix Stock was worth a lot of money, and he looked the part. But behind a pair of wire-framed glasses, his green eyes were those of a very worried man.

Stock smiled at the Hardys and Chet. "I'm really

8

glad you could come out here," he said, shaking hands with the three teens.

Joe smiled back at the engineer, but he was having a hard time keeping his eyes off Stock's sports car.

Unlike most auto paint jobs, the Saurion's did not have a mirror finish. It appeared to have been burnished to a dull sheen. The hood was long, and the back end of the car short. There was a small winged dragon in a circle logo on the hood, and the windshield and windows were black, making it impossible to see into the Saurion's interior.

"It's amazing," Joe said.

"It's not a jeep," Chet said, grinning, "but it's not bad."

"Thanks, guys," Felix Stock said. "You're among the very few who have had a chance to see the Saurion. Just this morning I had to call security about a photographer who was trying to climb the fence at the back of the speedway." He took a small device that resembled a TV remote control from his pocket, pushed a button, and the driver's door clicked open.

Chet's eyebrows shot up. "No door handles."

"Door handles break the smooth flow of the design," Felix Stock explained. He pushed another button, and the opaque windshield and windows gradually lightened to clear glass.

"I've never seen Curt when he wasn't wearing

9

sunglasses," Felix Stock said, "but he won't need them in a Saurion. The entire top, including the windshield area and the roof, is made of light-sensitive material."

"You mean like those glasses that turn dark when you go out into the sunlight?" Joe asked.

"It's similar," Stock replied with a nod, "except that my new PEST system—that stands for Photo-electric Sensitive Top—is controllable from this remote or with several switches on the instrument panel. Or, if the driver prefers, he can set the system on automatic, and it will adjust the outside light. There is nothing like it anywhere."

"Pretty high-tech," Frank said.

"And potentially worth a fortune," Curt Kiser pointed out.

"That's why it's been kept super-secret," Stock said. "We don't want any competitors or industrial spies to get hold of the technology."

"Listen, since Curt and I have already seen this mechanical marvel," Jason Dain said, "we'd better excuse ourselves and get back to work. Saturday night's race is only two days off."

After Kiser and Dain had left the building, Stock turned to the three teens. "You ready to give the Saurion a test drive?" he asked.

"If you insist," Joe said casually, trying to hide his excitement.

Frank flipped a coin to see who would sit behind

10

the wheel first. Joe called heads, then grinned widely when Frank shrugged and said, "You win."

Stock handed Joe two helmets and the remote device. "There's no key and no ignition switch," he told the younger Hardy. "Once you've fastened your safety belt, push the Start button. After that, you operate it just like you would any other high-performance sports car."

Frank took one of the helmets and slipped into the passenger seat. "Remember, now," he told Joe as he adjusted his helmet, "you drive it for five minutes, then it's my turn."

"You hope," Joe replied. Joe fastened his seat belt and pressed the Start button. He had driven a few sports cars, but none had throbbed with the horsepower he felt humming smoothly under the burnished red hood.

Cocooned in the Saurion's deep leather seat, Joe felt as though he were wearing the car, and he could feel it move with the slightest touch of the leather-wrapped steering wheel. He eased the Saurion out onto the speedway's back straightaway. After looking both ways and finding it clear, Joe put the gas pedal to the floor at the same instant he let out the clutch. The Saurion took off like a rocket.

Joe felt a chill race down his spine. He had never before felt such power. A glance at the needles and numbers on the analog dial showed him that he was already running at 127 miles per hour.

11

"This machine is awesome!" Joe exclaimed.

"I don't mean to sound like Aunt Gertrude," Frank said, "but the needle just passed a hundred and thirty-five."

As the Saurion roared out of the third turn and headed into the front straightaway, Joe took his foot off the gas.

"We're not slowing down," Joe said with a frown. He pressed on the brake. The Saurion was still accelerating.

"Use the brakes," Frank suggested.

"I did." Joe tried the brakes again, pressing gently at first. When the car didn't slow, he pushed hard on the pedal.

"I can't slow it down," Joe said, alarm in his voice. "We're pushing a hundred and fifty."

"Can you downshift?" Frank asked urgently.

"Frank!" Joe gasped from behind the Saurion's steering wheel as the car began to fishtail. "I've lost control of this thing. It's like it's driving itself!"

Frank grabbed the remote device. Aiming it at the dashboard, he pushed the Ignition/Off button. Nothing happened.

"Stay calm," Frank warned. "We're not the only ones on the track."

Joe glanced out the Saurion's windshield at the racecourse ahead. A maintenance truck had pulled onto the track. It was cutting diagonally across the Saurion's path, heading slowly toward the side of the course.

12

Joe knew in an instant that if neither the truck nor the Saurion changed course, a horrible collision was going to occur. It was only a matter of seconds till the deathblow.

"Joe!" Frank shouted. "You've got to stop this car!"

2 Stolen Car

Joe looked through the Saurion's windshield at the maintenance truck. It was heading toward a gap in the wall that led between two spectator stands. It couldn't be moving at more than fifteen miles per hour, Joe calculated, as the truck grew rapidly larger before his eyes.

"Brace yourself!" Joe shouted. He pushed the gear lever hard to the right, then rammed the lever up into reverse. In that same instant he popped the clutch. Joe cringed when he heard the transmission's wrenching crack.

When Frank heard the screeching tires and felt the Saurion jerk into a skid, he knew his brother's tactic had worked. By locking up the car's transmis-

14

sion, the mangled drivetrain was serving as a substitute set of brakes.

"Missed him!" Joe exclaimed as the Saurion slid past the maintenance truck at an angle. He steered the sports car toward the outer wall around the track.

When he saw the flashing lights of a speedway tow truck approaching, Frank removed his helmet, released his seat belt, and opened the door.

"You guys all right?" Felix Stock called to them from the back of the truck. He was holding a large fire extinguisher. "When it looked like you were losing control, I thought we'd better get out here."

Chet, leaning out the truck's passenger side window, smiled when he saw the Hardys climb out of the Saurion unhurt. "It's a good thing Aunt Gertrude didn't see that," he said.

"We're okay," Joe said, "but there's something wrong with this car. It accelerated even after I took my foot off the gas."

"And Joe said the brakes stopped working," Frank added.

"Let's tow it back to the garage," Stock said, signaling to the driver of the wrecker, who skillfully and quickly hooked up the Saurion. The brothers and Chet rode back to Building A on the truck's back deck.

After the car was rolled into place, Stock examined it briefly. Then he led the Hardys and Chet to a small office in the back of the building.

15

"Let me fill you in on the problems here," Felix Stock said as he sat behind his desk. "It started with a threatening phone call."

"What did the caller say?" Frank asked.

"He called the Saurion a death car. He said whoever drove it would die a horrible death."

"Did you recognize the voice?" Joe inquired.

Stock shook his head. "At first I didn't really take the threat very seriously. But two weeks ago the Saurion nearly crushed me when one of the hydraulic jacks holding up its front end gave way. When I checked out the system, I discovered the oil in the lines had been drained."

"Couldn't it have just been a leak?" Joe asked.

"There would have been oil on the floor, or in the corner where the jacks are stored. I looked, and there wasn't any. Then someone broke into my office safe and rummaged through the plans for the Saurion. Several important wiring diagrams are missing. That's when I decided to call your father. He said you two could help me."

"If these are the famous Hardy brothers, they probably can," said a woman behind them. The Hardys and Chet turned and saw a young woman with blue eyes and long blond hair that was tied back with a red silk scarf. She stood just outside the doorway, smiling at Frank and Joe.

"I've read a lot about you in the newspapers. My name is Katie Bratton," she said. "I'm Felix's test driver."

"And she's one of the best," Felix Stock added. "When someone wants a new racing car pushed to the limit to see what it'll do, Katie's the driver. She's been with the Saurion project since the beginning. And she'll be at the wheel on the race Saturday night."

"Did you drive the Saurion?" Katie asked the Hardys.

"We ran it around the track a couple of times," Joe said, smiling at Katie. She was a small woman. Joe guessed that she was about five feet, barely tall enough to see over the steering wheel.

"Did you ever have any trouble with the way it handled?" Frank asked Katie.

"The Saurion's absolutely the best tracking car on the road," she answered. "It doesn't pull. It won't even vibrate, and we're talking at about two hundred miles an hour." A puzzled expression came over her face. "Why, is it out of alignment or something?"

Frank told Katie about their experience on the track.

"You dropped the transmission?" Katie said, frowning at Joe.

"I probably only tore out a gear or two," Joe admitted sheepishly.

"Actually, you tore out all six," Felix Stock said. "It'll need a whole new transmission."

"Are you always that hard on your cars?" Katie asked Joe.

17

"Of course not," Joe replied. "Like my brother said, the Saurion was totally out of control."

Katie nodded thoughtfully. "It's never done anything like that." She paused for a moment, then said, "As Felix has probably told you, there have been some very strange things going on around here." She handed Joe a folded piece of paper. "I found this in my locker when I got here today."

Joe opened the note and saw that it was made up of letters cut from newspapers. " 'The faster you drive,' " Joe read aloud, " 'the sooner you die!' "

"Someone's idea of a joke," Katie said with a shrug. Frank noticed that she didn't sound scared at all.

"That's the last straw," Felix announced, turning to Katie. "You may think these incidents are practical jokes, but I don't. There's not going to be any race. I can't let you risk it."

"Come on, Felix," Katie said firmly. "You're not going to back down now, after all you've been through to get the Saurion ready."

"I am if someone is really trying to sabotage the car," Stock said stubbornly. "I'm going to call Mr. Ota over at Miyagi Motors and suggest we postpone the race."

"That's exactly what the person who's behind these threats wants you to do," Frank pointed out. "Why don't you let us do a little investigating first. This is only Thursday."

"If you cancel now," Joe added, "whoever is doing these things will stop. The more threats or sabotage attempts, the more likely he'll be to trip himself up."

"I'm no detective," Katie said, "but if I were looking for someone who might want to sabotage the Saurion, I'd choose that project engineer over at Miyagi Motors."

"What makes you think it's him?" Frank asked.

"I've met the guy," she replied. "His name is Takeo Ota. He sounded to me as if he was against having the race."

"That wasn't my impression," Felix Stock said. "He told me he was looking forward to the race."

"I'm convinced Mr. Ota's afraid his Sata Speedster will lose," Katie insisted. "And a loss would hurt Miyagi's sales."

"We'll talk to him," Joe told Katie.

"I'm not going to let an accident and a couple of dumb pranks scare me off," Katie said to Stock.

Felix Stock pointed to the note in Joe's hand. "As far as I'm concerned, this is a death threat," he said firmly.

"It's also a clue," Joe pointed out. "Do you mind if I hold on to it for a while?"

Katie nodded. Then she said evenly, "Look, Felix, I drove race cars while I was in high school. I've driven for ten years. I've been in accidents and pileups, and as you can plainly see, I'm perfectly all

19

right. I *refuse* to let some rival car manufacturer scare me out of one of the biggest races of the year. And I don't think you should let yourself get scared off, either."

"Okay, okay," Stock said with a sigh. "Maybe you're right."

"Why don't you show us around your area here at the speedway?" Frank said. "I'd like to take a look at that hydraulic jack."

Stock got up from behind his desk and motioned for the group to follow him out of the office.

"Were these the original Gasoline Alley garages?" Frank asked as they passed the three buildings that made up the Stock Motor Car Company.

"That's right," Stock replied. "The garages you see down this roadway were built back when the speedway was new." He gestured toward the aging brick and wooden structures.

Frank noticed broken panes in some of the windows. Many of the wooden frames and doors needed painting.

"Ticket sales haven't been too good here at the track," Stock told them. "If my company weren't using these three buildings, they'd just be standing idle. The speedway's newer garages are around the fourth turn and behind the starting line and viewing stands. They're much more convenient for the drivers and their mechanics. They even have their own underpasses beneath the racetrack to the pit area."

"Do you pay Kiser for the use of the garages?" Joe asked.

"Felix doesn't pay any rent," Katie said.

As the group approached Building C, Chet stopped and gave a low whistle. "Look at all these Saurions!"

"We use a carbon fiber body," Felix Stock explained, leading the group into the garage. "That means the Saurion's frame is made out of a composite material rather than steel. It's ten times stronger but a lot lighter."

"It's state of the art," Katie said proudly.

Frank counted a dozen cars in various stages of production. All of them had complete drivetrains, and several wore their finished body panels, ready for painting.

"I have orders for all of these cars," Stock told the Hardys and Chet. "In fact, if it didn't take so much handcrafting to build each one, I could sell ten times this many."

"That's not the idea, though," Katie said. "He's not making hamburgers. Felix wants quality, not quantity."

"I see no one's working on the cars today," Frank noted. "Are you building these by yourself?"

Stock shook his head. "I gave everyone except Marvin some time off while we got through race weekend," Stock explained. "Marvin Tarpley's my best mechanic. He's the only one who can touch the car, except Katie, of course. He's around here somewhere. He also works for the demolition der-by." Stock led them over to a corner of the shop. "There's the jack," he said, pointing.

Taking a small penlight from his pocket, Joe knelt down and examined the hydraulic jack. He recognized it as an old model. The red paint on the cast-iron body had long ago chipped and faded.

"There are fresh scratches on this oil coupling," he said. "I'd say someone disconnected the tube and bled the system."

"How about the people who work for you?" Frank asked. "Do you trust them all?"

"I don't actually know them personally," Stock said thoughtfully, "except for Katie here." Katie smiled.

"Could you give us a list of your employees?" Frank asked. "We need to check them out."

"Let's go on back to my office, and I'll get it for you. Then I'd better find Marvin to help me repair the prototype."

Frank took a last look around the assembly building. Suddenly he spotted a small object lying on the floor. He picked it up and glanced at it quickly. It was made of plastic, but Frank couldn't identify it. He slipped it into his pocket and hurried out of the garage behind his brother.

Chet and Katie were in the lead as the group approached the large overhead door leading into Building A.

"Oh, no!" Katie exclaimed as she stepped out of the sun into the dimness of the garage.

"What's wrong now?" Felix Stock demanded.

"Everything!" Katie Bratton gasped. "The Saurion's gone!"

3 Buried Alive

"Don't touch anything," Joe Hardy ordered, looking around the empty garage, where the Saurion had been parked only minutes before.

"How could this happen?" Katie said in disbelief.

"I'm finished," Felix Stock said with a groan.

"There's a rational explanation for this," Frank said to Stock. "Cars don't just disappear."

"It couldn't have been driven out of here," Chet said. "We would have heard it."

"And if someone towed it, we would have heard that noise, too. We weren't so far away," Joe added.

"Maybe it was pushed," Frank said. "We left the overhead door open. Pushing it wouldn't have made much noise."

"But where was it pushed?" Felix Stock asked in an exasperated tone. "And how far could anyone push it?"

Joe studied the concrete floor where the Saurion had been parked. "There aren't any tracks," he announced, gazing around the room.

He noticed an overhead door at the back of the garage. Crates had been piled up against it. "There's a fine coating of dust on the floor at the back and sides of the garage, and there aren't even tracks from when we drove the Saurion in. It looks to me like the floor has been swept."

"I'm going to call the main gate to see if the guard has seen the Saurion," Stock announced. He headed for his office at the back of the building. Katie stayed with the Hardys and Chet.

Frank took the small plastic object out of his pocket and handed it to his brother. "I found this in Building C, back in the corner where Stock keeps his jacks," Frank said. "Got any idea what it is?"

Turning toward the outside light, Joe studied the matchbook-size piece of black plastic. He noticed several color-coded wires coming out of one end. Joe shrugged. "Your guess is as good as mine," he said. "But let's hold on to it. It could be a clue."

Just then, Stock walked back over to them. "No one has entered or left the speedway grounds in the past half hour," he announced. He handed Frank a printout that listed his current employees.

"That means the Saurion is still here somewhere, probably hidden nearby," Frank said.

Joe held up the black plastic object Frank had found and asked Stock, "Is this a part out of the Saurion?"

Frowning, Stock studied the tiny piece of plastic. "No," he said. "I've never seen it before."

"It's definitely not just a doodad," Chet said, looking over Felix Stock's shoulders. "Could be a gizmo or a widget."

"How would we ever solve any cases without you?" Joe said with a sigh.

"Actually, we need your help right now," Frank told Chet. "Joe and I are going to search the grounds for the Saurion. While we do that, you take the gizmo around and ask every mechanic and driver you see if they can identify it."

"You can use my golf cart," Felix Stock said quickly, noticing the pained look on Chet's face. "It might take you a while to walk around the grounds."

"If you want to find the car," Katie Bratton said knowingly, "I'd start at Miyagi Motors."

"That's a serious accusation," Joe said quietly. "Do you have any evidence?"

"If you work around auto racing," Katie said, untying her red silk scarf and combing her hair with her fingers, "you hear things."

"Things like what?" Frank asked.

26

"Just talk, mostly out at the Circuit Diner," she said. "It's up on Shore Road."

"The Circuit's a hangout for race drivers and the guys over at Kiser's demolition derby," Stock explained.

"A diner," Chet said, his face brightening. "Why don't we start our investigating over there?"

Joe ignored Chet's suggestion. "Is there a backup car for the race?" he asked Stock.

"No prototype, no race," Felix replied sadly. "And without that race, I'm afraid the Saurion will be a dud. I was counting on the publicity from the race to launch the car onto the market." He rubbed his forehead slowly. "Unless Marvin, Katie, and I can prepare one of those production models," he said.

"We can do it," Katie insisted.

Joe handed Chet the plastic block and said, "You know what you have to do."

"Right," Chet said as he jogged toward a golf cart parked in front of the building.

"Okay, let's search the area," Frank said in a determined tone.

When they stepped outside the garage, Joe bent down and inspected the aged blacktop paving. Frank examined the small grassy area in between the buildings.

"No tracks," Joe reported a few moments later.

"And no footprints, either," Frank added.

27

"Do you think there's anything to Katie's idea that Miyagi Motors is behind Stock's problems?" Joe asked. "Or behind what happened on the course this morning?"

"It's too early to say," Frank replied. "But when we get home, we can look for prints on the note Katie received. And when we finish here, we should check out the Circuit Diner. In the meantime, there are garages all over Gasoline Alley. And there are a lot of trailer trucks parked around here. We should check those out, too."

"You take the trucks, and I'll work the buildings," Joe suggested.

Frank headed for the nearest truck, a black trailer bearing the crest of a famous Indy car racing team. The doors were locked, and there was no way of seeing inside. It would have been impossible to load the Saurion in the trailer without pushing the car across some grass, Frank figured, and there was no indication that anything or anyone had been on the unmowed grass. Frank thought the grass looked bedraggled compared with the lawn at the Hardys' home.

He studied the grass more closely and noticed a browned-out area between buildings B and C. When he walked around B to Building A, he saw another brown patch in the space between those two buildings. The burned-out strip was about eight feet wide.

"Why would the grass on the sides of the buildings be green," Frank muttered, "and the strips in the middle nearly dead?" He knelt down and felt the soil. It was dry. "And why is the edge along the brown area so straight?" he added to himself.

Meanwhile, Joe was looking around Building C. When Stock and Katie arrived from Stock's office, Joe lent them a hand moving one of the partially built Saurion's from its place in line.

"This silver one is closest to being fully assembled," Stock said.

"Don't worry, Felix," Katie said firmly. "One car or the other, I'll win that race."

Joe thought Felix Stock's smile was forced, but the hug the engineer gave his driver was sincere enough.

"I hate to interrupt," Joe said, clearing his throat, "but what's in Building B? The door was closed when we passed it."

"That's our parts department," Stock told him. "It's a warehouse, really. I can't imagine there would be any place to hide the prototype there, but you're welcome to look." He handed Joe the keys.

Joe unlocked a side entrance to Building B, then flipped the light switch inside the door. The only sound in the room came from the door clicking shut behind him. Building B contained row after row of wooden and metal shelving. Joe stared at the mass of fenders, frames, alternators, frame sections, and cardboard boxes of all sizes that filled the shelves.

Although he doubted he would find the car, Joe

29

began a systematic search. Slowly he walked around the interior of the huge building. Finding nothing, he began to walk down the aisles between the shelves.

Suddenly Joe stopped. In the vast stillness of the warehouse, he heard something. Slowly he turned toward the sound, but detected nothing.

"Must have been a mouse," he said to himself as he continued down the aisle.

Crack!

It wasn't very loud, but it was the sound of a piece of glass or ceramic being crushed. Joe froze in place, and as he did, the lights went out. Joe was enveloped in blackness.

He reached silently for his penlight. As he did, from across the room came the sound of straining metal, then a resounding crash. He knew one of the long shelves weighed down by parts had been knocked against its neighbor across the aisle.

A second loud crash followed. A sickening fear came over Joe as he realized that the shelves, like a row of dominoes, were falling onto each other.

Joe turned and ran back toward the other end of the aisle he had been searching. Pointing the slim flashlight, he frantically searched for the light switch. He found it and flicked it on.

The beam of light gave Joe a quick glimpse of the metal shelving as it leaned into the aisle next to him. He looked up and saw a car battery falling off the shelf just over his head. He threw his arms up to protect himself and turned to run away, but it was too late. Bins of bolts and nuts, engine parts, and suspension arms showered down on him, and he crumpled to the floor under the heavy pile.

Frank was about to enter a small storage shed attached to the back of Building B when he heard a series of crashing noises coming from the huge warehouse. He hurried over to the building, wondering fearfully if Joe was inside.

"Joe!" he called, glancing hurriedly around the area. "Where are you?"

Frank didn't see his brother or hear an answer. He rushed up to the overhead door and found that it was securely locked. Darting around to the side door, he saw that it, too, was locked.

"I think Joe's inside!" Frank cried as Felix Stock and Katie Bratton came running up to him.

"We heard the crashes," Stock said.

"Use my key," Katie offered, rummaging in the pocket of her suit.

Frank quickly unlocked the door, then pushed it open. The interior of the building was pitch black.

"Joe!" Frank called out. "Are you in here?"

The three waited for an answer, but there was only silence. Felix Stock flipped the light switch. Katie Bratton gasped.

As the fluorescent tubes blinked on, Frank looked out on a sea of disaster. An entire row of shelves, from one side of the warehouse to the other, lay on

31

the floor. The metal was buckled and bent, and heavy auto parts and countless smaller parts were spilled all over the floor.

Frank stopped and signaled the others to be quiet. Listening closely, he heard a moan coming from somewhere in the middle of the pile of debris.

"He's buried under those shelves," Frank said as he scrambled over the twisted metal and boxes. "Joe, where are you?"

"Over here," came Joe's muffled reply.

Frank followed the sound of Joe's voice. When he reached the area, he began moving auto parts and shelving aside carefully. He didn't want to start another avalanche of falling equipment.

Finally he saw his brother's face looking up at him.

"Whew!" Joe said. "That was a close one."

"If it hadn't been for this grille wedged under the shelf," Frank said, "the full weight of it would have fallen on top of you. Are you okay?"

"Just get me out of here," Joe said, rubbing a painful lump on the side of his head.

Stock and Katie kept the shelf from falling while Frank pulled Joe out.

"This was no accident," Joe said once he was back on his feet. "The lights went out, and the next thing I knew, the shelves were caving in."

"I was right outside when I heard the crashes," Frank said. "If someone had come out, I would have seen him."

"I was outside facing the side door," Katie said. "I didn't see anyone, either."

"Is there any other way out of here?" Frank asked, looking around the wrecked warehouse.

"Not that I know of," Stock said. "There's just the overhead and the side door."

"Then he's still got to be here," Joe said in a low voice. "But where?"

"Let's split up and search," Frank whispered. "We'll meet back at the side door."

Five minutes later the four of them gathered by the door.

"Nobody else is in here," Katie said.

"I can't believe this," Stock said. "If someone pushed over the shelves, where is he?"

"I don't know, but someone is definitely responsible," Joe insisted. "Before the lights went out, I heard a crack, as if someone had stepped on a piece of glass."

Frank scanned the warehouse again. He looked up and saw two grimy skylights set into the ceiling. "Someone could have shinnied up those standpipes against the wall and gotten out through the roof."

Frank led the group out the door and around Building B's outer walls, looking for a way to get up on the roof.

Joe glanced up at the sound of a whining electric motor. It was Chet in the golf cart.

"Nobody knows what it is," Chet announced, holding up the small plastic part. "I even showed it

33

to Curt Kiser and Jason Dain. I thought Kiser recognized it because he kept staring at it, but finally he said that it had nothing to do with the speedway."

"Thanks," Frank told Chet, taking the small piece of plastic from his friend. "Did you by any chance see a ladder anywhere?"

"We want to get up on that roof," Joe explained. He told his friend what had happened in the warehouse.

"I've got a ladder over in the shop," Stock said. He turned to Chet. "Would you give me a hand with it? It's kind of heavy."

When the ladder was placed against the side of the building, Joe scrambled up the rungs. Slowly he peeked over the edge. "No one here," he called down.

Frank followed his brother up while Chet stayed on the ground with Katie and Felix to steady the ladder.

Joe took one half of the roof area, Frank the other, and they scoured the gravel and tarred surface for footprints and clues.

"Nothing," Joe admitted. "There's no sign that anyone's been up here for years."

"Find anything?" Chet yelled up from the foot of the ladder. "I mean, if there's nothing up there, maybe we could . . ." His voice trailed off.

"You wouldn't be getting hungry, would you?" Frank called down to him.

34

"I was thinking maybe we could take a break for lunch," Chet replied.

"Get the jeep," Joe said, backing down the ladder.

While Frank told Stock and Katie to keep their eyes open, Joe assured them that he and Frank would get to the bottom of the Saurion's disappearance. Five minutes later Chet pulled up in his jeep.

"You sure that antique shouldn't be in a museum?" Felix asked Chet as he looked over the battered, rusty vehicle.

Frank and Joe laughed as they climbed in the jeep. Chet ignored his friends' laughter. Instead he asked Stock directions to the Circuit Diner.

"Didn't Katie say the Circuit is where all the race car drivers hang out?" Chet asked as he guided the jeep out of the main gate and onto Shore Road.

"Right," Joe said. "Maybe we can pick up some information about the case there."

When they pulled into the parking lot of the diner, Frank said, "Look at the customers' cars. Every one of them is waxed and polished."

Inside, Joe led the group past a long counter with a row of swivel stools in front of it. He headed for one of two empty booths along the side wall.

Frank glanced around at the customers. Most of them were men in jeans and T-shirts. Frank guessed they had been working on their cars. The two men in the booth next to them looked particularly grimy.

Frank got up to get a third table setting from the

counter. On his way back he got a better look at the men in the next booth. The dark-haired man with his back to Joe and Chet's seat wore torn, grease-stained jeans, black leather boots, and leather bands on both wrists. He was short and muscular. The other man had light brown hair and was thin and wiry.

After the three placed their orders, Frank looked at Chet and asked, "You and Curt Kiser studied that electronic part carefully, right?"

Chet nodded. "And Jason Dain hardly glanced at it," Chet replied. "He told me right off it wasn't anything that went in any car he'd ever seen." Chet paused while he looked over at the grill to see how their lunches were coming. "I didn't come away empty-handed, though," he added with a grin. "Kiser did give me passes to the demolition derby tomorrow. You want to go?"

"Sure, we'll probably be on the grounds, any-way," Frank said, "especially if we don't find the Saurion soon."

The waitress brought the orders of burgers and fries the three friends had ordered.

Joe was putting ketchup on his fries when the voices coming from the next booth caught his attention. Frank glanced up to see Joe freeze in midmotion.

"What's wrong?" Frank whispered.

Joe leaned back against the vinyl, straining to hear more.

36

"Is something wrong?" Chet finally asked.

"I'm not sure," Joe said in a low voice. "The guys behind us are talking about a car race. I didn't hear any names, but one of the guys said that if she goes through with it, it'll be the last race she'll ever run."

"You sure you heard him say 'she'?" Frank whispered.

Joe nodded grimly. "Yeah, and another thing. He called the car the Death Car."

Frank frowned. "Stock received a warning with those same words, remember? These guys could be tied in to what's been happening on the speedway."

"Do you think one of these guys pushed over those shelves?" Chet asked.

Joe silenced Chet while he listened to the voices in the booth behind him.

After a moment Joe said, "I don't know, but what they're saying about the race is more important right now. They're saying that if Katie Bratton races the Saurion on Saturday, she's going to die."

4 The Runaway Robot

Joe got up from his seat.

"Where are you going?" Chet asked.

"I'm just going to do a little investigating," Joe told him in a low voice. "I want to get a look at the guys in the next booth."

Joe hurried over to the counter. "I'd like another soda," he told the waitress.

"Sure, it'll be right out," she answered through a wad of chewing gum.

As he walked back, Joe stared boldly at the two men. Their conversation stopped abruptly, and the short, stocky man looked up at Joe. The other man, who was finishing a piece of cherry pie, remained silent.

"Hey, kid, what are you staring at?" the stocky man snapped.

Joe noticed that the man needed a shave and his mouth was twisted into a scowl. "Sorry," Joe said pleasantly. "I thought I recognized you."

"Well, you were wrong," the man growled.

But Joe wasn't ready to give up. "Don't you work out at the speedway? I've seen you at the demolition derby."

"Keep it up," the man warned, "and you'll be seeing stars." He laughed at his own threat. "Now get lost."

"Okay, okay," Joe said, holding up his hands. "My mistake." He walked away as the two men got up, sauntered over to the counter, and paid their check.

As they left the restaurant, Joe went to the front window. He watched the stocky man get into a brand-new white panel truck and drive away. Joe jotted down the license number. The thin, brown-haired man left on a motorcycle.

"While you were ordering that soda," Frank said when Joe sat down again, "the thin one told the short guy that if he was serious about getting work at Miyagi Motors with this scheme, he'd end up in the state pen."

Before Joe could comment, the waitress brought his soda. He slid it over to Chet.

Joe walked back over to the counter. Sounding

39

like the world's biggest racing fan, Joe asked the waitress, "Weren't those guys the famous Indy car drivers Henry Conlon and Bob Lynd?"

"Nah," the waitress said. "Those guys are from the demo derby. I don't know their names. All I know is that one guy is the mechanic. The other drives. And they never tip."

Joe returned to the booth and sat down. He told Frank and Chet what the waitress had said.

"Do you think those guys are behind the sabotage?" Chet asked.

"Could be," Frank said thoughtfully. "Katie was saying that someone out at Miyagi Motors was behind it," he added. "As long as we're this close, let's head over to Miyagi Motors and have a look around."

"You just want to see your girlfriend," Chet said to Frank in a teasing tone. "Isn't she interning at Miyagi Motors?"

"That's right," Joe said. "Callie is completing a business internship there."

"I'll give her a call and see if she can set up a meeting with Takeo Ota," Frank said.

While Chet and Joe paid the check, Frank used the pay phone to call Callie.

"The Miyagi plant has been open about a year," Joe said as Chet turned the jeep onto the road that led to the sprawling Miyagi Motors Assembly Center.

Located north of Bayport and the speedway, the

40

four-acre building complex was as sleek and uncluttered as the cars Miyagi was famous for designing. The only break Joe could see in the straight horizontal lines of the one-story factory was a block of windows in the center of the first floor.

"Miyagi's very successful," Frank commented as Chet braked to a halt at the guardhouse just outside the main gate. "The paper says they sell every sedan they make."

"Mr. Ota is expecting you," the guard told them after Frank explained they had an appointment.

When the jeep entered the visitor parking lot next to the managerial offices, Frank could see Callie Shaw standing next to a Miyagi sedan. Her blond hair shone in the sun, and she was smiling. With her was a Japanese man.

The Hardys and Chet got out of the jeep and walked up to Callie and the man. Frank saw that the man was wearing a yellow hard hat and identification tag on his white shirt.

"Allow me to introduce myself," the man said. "I am Takeo Ota. I am the project engineer for our new sports car, the Sata Speedster."

"Mr. Ota is my supervisor while I'm here at Miyagi," Callie explained.

"Welcome to Miyagi," Mr. Ota added. "It is a pleasure to have you visit. Please follow us in your car."

Mr. Ota and Callie got into the sedan. Frank admired the curving lines of the car, then got into the jeep with his friends. Joe helped Chet force the gearshift into first so they could keep up with the sedan.

"I read that this building is a half mile long," Frank said as they neared the factory.

"Did that article say anything about Miyagi using unmarked panel trucks?" Joe asked. He pointed to a white truck parked in the lot. "That tough guy at the diner was driving a panel truck just like that one."

"We can check on it later," Frank said.

Chet parked beside the sedan. Then they all followed Mr. Ota into the factory. Joe took the visitor tags from Mr. Ota and handed two to Frank and Chet.

"I am sure you will enjoy looking at the Speedster," Mr. Ota said confidently as he led them down a long hall and through a doorway to the main assembly room.

The room was huge and contained two steadily moving lines. One, Frank saw, carried drivetrain assemblies. Along the other, sedan frames paraded one by one, each receiving its own engine, transmission, and rear axle.

"This assembly line is as clean as an operating room," Frank said to Mr. Ota.

"And safe, too," Mr. Ota reported over the noise of the line. "And to keep it that way, please put on these hard hats and protective goggles." Callie handed out the equipment to her friends.

Joe watched as the separate sections of sedan frames were grasped by a robotic arm from rows of components on both sides of the line.

"Wow," Chet said. "Are these what they call industrial robots?"

"That's right," Mr. Ota replied. "They might not look human, but each robotic arm duplicates human movements. One difference between robots and humans, though, is that robots are tireless."

"That means no lunch break," Joe said, grinning at Chet.

"The new Speedster is down this way," Mr. Ota said, leading the four teens along the line.

"Watch your head," Callie warned as they crossed under the assembly line through a narrow wire cage underpass.

"Beautiful!" Frank said in an awed tone when he saw the bright yellow Sata Speedster parked in the center of the cavernous design studio.

Joe nodded in agreement. The Saurion might look more futuristic, but he thought the Speedster had a more balanced design. With its engine housed in its rear end, the body flowed forward smoothly into an aerodynamically angled nose.

"Felix Stock said the Saurion is made out of some kind of composite material," Chet said. "Is this one plastic, too?"

Mr. Ota smiled gently. "I know Felix Stock very well. His new model is a fine machine, in many ways much more advanced than the Speedster. Each

43

Saurion is being built mostly by hand, but we cannot do that here. We designed the Speedster so it could be built on an assembly line. Even so, the Speedster has a magnesium frame with an aluminum skin," he explained. "Many actual racing cars are built from the same materials. It makes our car very light."

"It should reach close to two hundred miles an hour on the straightaways Saturday night," Callie said.

"Let me ask you something, Mr. Ota," Frank said. "Why do you want to race Mr. Stock?"

"The publicity," Mr. Ota said quickly. "In the automobile's early days, that is one of the ways the different companies established themselves. Miyagi Motors is a small company, and we are new in your country. Even if we lose to the Saurion, we will get a lot of publicity. Besides," he added, smiling broadly, "I really enjoy a good car race."

Frank and Joe exchanged glances. "Then you really want this race," Joe said.

"Of course I do!" Mr. Ota replied enthusiastically. Then he frowned. "Has anyone suggested anything to the contrary?"

"There have been a bunch of weird incidents over at the speedway," Chet blurted out. "Frank and Joe are just looking around for Felix Stock."

"People aren't saying *I* have had anything to do with that?" Mr. Ota asked, looking concerned.

44

"No, Mr. Ota," Frank said quickly. "Of course not."

"Well, I did *not!*" the project engineer said emphatically. "And if anyone at Miyagi Motors were involved in such a thing, they would be released."

"We believe you," Joe said to Mr. Ota in a reassuring tone.

The Hardys, Callie, and Chet followed Mr. Ota back through the short tunnel to the far side of the assembly line.

"Soon every tenth car coming down this line will be the Sata Speedster," Mr. Ota said, beaming. "It's going to take a tremendous amount of coordination. When a different model comes by, the robots will have to adjust their movements."

"How does a robot know what car's next?" Chet asked, stopping beside one of the robot arms. "Do these things have brains?"

"Not exactly," Mr. Ota said. "They are controlled by computers, which have to be preprogrammed before production can begin. It's been done in only one other auto assembly plant." He paused while one of the long arms slithered past overhead, tilted, then dropped its mechanical hand into a bin containing windshield assemblies. "The arm is equipped with sensors," the engineer continued, "that are wired into interlocks so the computer can tell when something is wrong. If there's a

45

problem, the computer immediately shuts down the arm."

"Very impressive," Frank said, stepping toward the line for a closer look at a second robotic arm, this one connected to a welding torch.

Joe turned to gaze at a shower of sparks coming from the parts being welded. Out of the corner of his eye he noticed something move swiftly. Glancing up, he saw that the long robotic arm that brought the windshield frames to the line had picked up another one. But instead of reaching in an arc well overhead, it was sweeping a full three feet lower, toward the group.

Joe saw that the arm was swinging directly at Frank's head. "Frank, watch it!" Joe shouted, lunging toward his brother.

But before Joe could reach Frank, the robot rotated swiftly on its well-lubricated bearings. Joe watched in horror as the mechanical arm slammed into Frank.

5 Off-Road Vehicle

The robotic arm knocked Frank off his feet and threw him into the frame on the assembly line.

"Stop the line!" Mr. Ota immediately cried out.

While buzzers sounded, Joe scrambled aboard the car frame where his brother lay still on his back.

Joe felt a jolt as the assembly line stopped. He grasped Frank around the waist and shoulders and began backing out. Chet rushed over to help.

"This is terrible, terrible," Mr. Ota said with a moan. "What could have gone wrong?"

Callie directed Joe and Chet toward a foreman's cubicle. "Put him down here," Callie said as she removed cushions from a chair and placed them on the floor.

Frank groaned as Joe, Chet, and Mr. Ota eased him onto the cushions. Then Callie removed Frank's hard hat.

"What hit me?" Frank asked in a groggy voice.

"You were decked by a robot," Chet told him.

Callie knelt down next to Frank and examined his head for any signs of a wound. "Are you all right?"

"I'll be fine," he assured her. "That arm must have glanced off my hard hat."

"It did," Chet said. He showed Frank the yellow plastic hard hat, and Frank saw that it was cracked.

"I am *very* sorry about this," Mr. Ota insisted. "There will be a thorough investigation before the line is started again. That arm never should have deviated from its programmed path."

"You're saying it was a computer error?" Joe asked. "Where is the computer?"

"I'll show you," Mr. Ota said.

While Callie and Chet stayed with Frank, Joe followed Mr. Ota up a steep metal stairway onto a platform. Against one wall was a bank of computers. Mr. Ota entered several passwords into one of the computers.

"The oil pressure on that arm is nearly zero," the engineer said. "There's probably a leak. I promise you, Joe, we will find out what happened."

When Joe and Mr. Ota went back downstairs to the cubicle, Frank was getting to his feet. "I'm feeling okay now," he told them. He turned to Mr. Ota. "Have you by any chance noticed a stocky,

48

muscular man who wears leather wristbands around here?" he asked the engineer. "He dresses like a mechanic. He might have been visiting someone in the office."

"Do you know his name?" Mr. Ota asked.

"No, we don't," Frank replied. "But we have reason to believe that he was here not too long ago. He may have applied for a job."

"We can check personnel," Mr. Ota suggested. "Every applicant and employee is photographed for the company ID badges, and we keep copies on file."

Mr. Ota led the group to the personnel office. There he asked a young clerk to bring three large binders to the counter. Frank, Joe, and Chet each took one. They looked through the records but found that none of the men in the photos resembled the man they had seen at the diner.

Joe closed his binder and looked at Ota. "Does your company use any white panel trucks?" he asked the engineer.

"Why, yes," Mr. Ota said. "The company very recently purchased ten vehicles like that. Why?"

"A person we suspect of sabotaging the Saurion was driving one," Joe told him.

"One of our trucks?" Mr. Ota asked, a shocked expression on his face.

"It's possible that someone here at Miyagi Motors doesn't want the race between your Speedster and the Saurion to happen," Joe said.

49

"But why?" Mr. Ota wanted to know. "I don't see how it could hurt us that much, even if we lose. Mass-production cars always do better in the marketplace than specialty cars like Stock's. He's the one who could be hurt by not having the race."

"That's why we're trying to help him out," Frank said.

"Would you be able to give us a list of license numbers for those trucks?" Joe asked.

"Of course," Takeo Ota said. He punched some commands into a computer, then some more. "For some reason they are not listed. But I'll see that you get them."

"Let's go home, then," Frank suggested, "and run that license number from the diner through the department of motor vehicles."

"And it is nearly quitting time for you, Ms. Shaw," Mr. Ota said to Callie, "so if you wish to leave with your friends, it's fine with me."

When the group reached the parking lot, Joe scanned the area for the unmarked panel truck. It was gone.

Callie climbed into the jeep's tattered passenger seat. Frank and Joe settled into the cargo area behind.

"The way I see it," Frank said as the jeep lurched away from Miyagi Motors, "Takeo Ota is definitely not behind the incidents at the speedway. He just doesn't strike me as a criminal. He was willing to show us the company records, and I don't think he has anything to gain by sabotaging the race."

"What about the robot arm?" Callie asked.

"It was probably just a malfunction," Frank replied.

"Then what have we got?" Joe asked. "We overheard two men talking in a diner, one of whom threatened a woman's life."

"And if that woman isn't Katie Bratton," Frank said, "it's one amazing coincidence."

"We have a license number," Joe continued, "and it would have been possible for the guy in the panel truck to get from Building B, where I was almost crushed, out to the restaurant before we got there."

"We've got a warning note and that little electronic device," Frank added. "First thing tomorrow we've got to get over to the electronic supplier and see what it is."

"If this car had a phone," Joe said, "we could check to see if the Saurion's turned up."

Chet glanced up at the rearview mirror and said, "Hey, guys. Look behind us."

"It's a white panel truck," Frank said grimly. "He's trying to catch up to us."

"How fast will this hunk of junk go?" Joe asked Chet.

"Not as fast as that truck," Chet admitted. "And it's a jeep, not a hunk of junk."

51

"It's too late, anyway," Frank announced as he watched the unmarked truck roaring up behind them.

"What do I do?" Chet asked, panic in his voice.

"Keep the jeep steady," Joe said as he looked back at the truck.

Callie gasped as the truck suddenly speeded up and pulled to within inches of the jeep's back bumper.

"Can you see the driver?" Joe asked his brother.

Frank squinted. "I think he's wearing a racing helmet," he said. "With the visor pulled down."

"Don't panic," Joe calmly told Chet as the truck pulled alongside the jeep.

"What's he doing?" Chet cried. "Is he going to try to run us off the road?"

A violent jolt to the jeep was Chet's answer, and the lightweight jeep was knocked to the shoulder.

"We're heading for the ditch!" Chet shouted as he slammed on the brakes. Despite Chet's efforts, the jeep slid down a steep embankment.

"Look out for that storm drain!" Joe called.

"I see it," Chet said. The drain was visible through the brush and trees that grew on the sides of the ditch.

Chet tried to regain control of the jeep. For an instant Frank thought he had it, but then he could feel the tires slip on some mud.

"Hang on!" Frank cried.

With a loud whack the front left side of the jeep slammed into the drain. Frank saw Chet lurch toward the windshield, his arms braced on the wheel for support.

Frank's heart skipped a beat when he saw that Callie wasn't in her seat. Then he spotted her. She'd been thrown out of the jeep and was lying dazed in the ditch, on top of some brush.

The Hardys and Chet jumped out of the jeep as its fall was halted by a tree.

"Callie, are you all right?" Frank asked when he reached the bottom of the slope. "Callie?"

"I'm okay," Callie said, pushing herself up on her elbows.

"You sure?" Frank asked, brushing dirt and leaves off Callie.

She assured him she was unharmed, but she was still a little shaken. "If I hadn't fallen in these bushes, I'd be in worse shape."

"Did you get the license number of that truck?" Joe asked his brother.

"No, it all happened too fast."

"First thing we do," Joe said firmly, "is push the jeep back up the slope."

"See if it will start," Frank said to Chet.

Chet turned the key. "Come on," he muttered between his teeth. Finally the engine sputtered to life, and he shifted into gear. Joe and Frank pushed the jeep up to level ground while Chet steered.

Within an hour the four teens were back in Bayport, parked in front of Callie's house.

"Thanks for the ride," Callie said as she climbed out of the jeep. "I'll see you guys at the demolition derby tomorrow night—although I don't know if I'm ready to see another car crash."

"See you tomorrow," Frank called out as Chet turned the jeep toward the Hardys' house.

When Frank and Joe stepped into their house, Aunt Gertrude was coming out of the kitchen. She stared at the brothers' muddy clothes. "Are you two all right?" she asked anxiously.

"Chet's jeep got stuck in a ditch," Joe said smoothly, glancing sideways at his brother. "We're fine."

"Well, at least you didn't get into an accident," Aunt Gertrude said.

"Hi, Dad," Frank said as he and Joe entered the book-lined study.

Fenton Hardy smiled at his sons. "Have you two been prospecting for mud?" he asked, raising his eyebrows. Joe filled his father in on the day's events.

"It looks as though the person who's behind Felix Stock's problems has found you," Fenton said. "Now you've got to find out who that person is.

"Felix called me late this afternoon," Fenton continued, "He said the Saurion is still missing."

"I don't think the Saurion left the speedway

grounds," Joe insisted. "We're going out there tomorrow morning and search again."

"Right now we want to run this license number through the department of motor vehicles," Frank said. "And we've got to identify this." He handed the small plastic device to his father.

"I'd say it's a relay switch," Fenton said, examining the device. "Relays can route electric currents onto some device, a motor for instance." He held the piece of plastic under the desk lamp. "What this particular one is used for, though, I don't know." He turned to his computer and punched in his private investigator ID number. "Go ahead and run that license number."

Frank keyed in the number, but the computer had no information on it.

"You copied the number down correctly?" Fenton asked.

"One-twelve JPA," Frank replied. "I was checking under truck licenses. Maybe they took the plate from a passenger car."

"Or an RV," Joe suggested.

"Nothing," Frank announced after checking.

"You seem to have found a license number that doesn't exist," Fenton said.

"I'm *sure* I wrote it down correctly," Frank insisted.

"Someone might have made that license plate," Fenton suggested.

"You think it's counterfeit?" Joe asked.

"It's possible. Someone with access to a machine shop could easily make his own plates."

"There are machine shops all over the speedway grounds," Frank said.

"And the waitress at the diner said the guys we saw there work at the demolition derby," Joe added.

Frank took a list from his pocket. "This is a printout of Stock's employees. We want to see if any of them have criminal records." Frank keyed in the names and Social Security numbers. Within seconds the information appeared on the screen.

"This is interesting," Joe said, looking closely at the screen. "Here's a guy who was given a lifetime suspension by a racing association. His name is Marvin Tarpley. He's been banned from driving in any of the races sponsored by the organization. Everyone else looks clean," he added.

"Didn't Stock say Tarpley was his best mechanic?" Frank asked.

Joe nodded. "We'll make a point of looking him up tomorrow," he said. Then he took the warning note from his pocket and showed it to his father.

"We want to check this for fingerprints," Joe said. "Katie Bratton, Stock's driver, found it in her locker this morning."

Fenton frowned as he looked at the note. "It's hard to raise prints on paper," he said.

The three checked the letter for prints using a

56

fingerprinting kit Joe brought in from the van. There were a few smudged prints but nothing clear enough to send to the police for checking.

"Do you think Mr. Ota has anything to do with the sabotage?" Fenton asked as he pondered the note.

"No," Joe said emphatically. "Mr. Ota wants that race."

"At least, he says he does," Frank said.

Aunt Gertrude called from the dining room, and the Hardys continued discussing the case over dinner.

Frank and Joe got up early Friday morning and had a quick breakfast before heading to Grayson's Electronics. Frank drove the van into downtown Bayport.

"Is Callie riding to the derby with us tonight?" Joe asked.

"Callie called last night after you went to bed. She said she'll meet us at the derby," Frank told his brother. "Remind me to leave her ticket at the pass gate."

Frank turned into the parking lot next to Grayson's Electronics, which was located on the edge of Bayport's waterfront. The store's plate-glass windows featured used radios, TVs, and VCRs.

"We've got a little mystery for you to solve," Joe said to Mr. Grayson as the brothers stepped into the shop.

"Could you tell us what this is used for?" Frank held up the plastic relay.

Mr. Grayson took the part and examined it closely. "What do you think it's for?" the electronics expert asked, looking back and forth at the two brothers.

"We thought it might have been used in a car," Joe told him, "maybe even an actual race car."

"You're right," Mr. Grayson said with a nod. "It is used in a car. This is what they call a power card. Two of these wires carry power from a battery, and these thicker wires connect up to motors or solenoids."

"What kind of car uses this?" Frank asked.

"A model car," Mr. Grayson said. "Radio control hobbyists use these. This particular power card is very expensive, nearly three hundred dollars."

"You mean remote control cars like those?" Joe said, pointing at the foot-long models on the shelves in back of Mr. Grayson.

"That's right," Mr. Grayson said. "The operator holds a remote, sort of like those joysticks used with video games. This little gem receives the signals from the remote." The technician handed the power card back to Frank. "Does that solve the mystery?" he asked.

"Not quite," Joe said with a smile. "But thanks for your help."

"So what do you think?" Frank asked as he slipped behind the wheel of the van. "Was the power card dropped in Building C by a mechanic who just happens to be a remote-control model car fan?"

"Maybe," Joe said thoughtfully.

The van's cellular phone buzzed, and Frank picked it up. "Hello?"

"I'm in big trouble!" he heard Chet say in a panicky voice. "I'm being held at the police station. They found a stolen car stereo in my jeep."

"Hang in there, we'll be right down," Frank said. He listened for a moment, while Chet told him more details about the stolen stereo, then hung up.

"What's going on?" Joe asked his brother.

"Chet's been arrested," Frank said.

"*Chet?* What for?"

"The police received an anonymous tip that a stereo had been stolen," Frank said as he pointed the van in the direction of the Bayport police station. "The caller even gave the police the license number of the thief's car. When they searched Chet's jeep, they found the stereo hidden under the seat. But that's not all," Frank added in a grim voice. "It's a stereo taken from the Saurion."

6 Broadsided

"I owe you guys one," Chet said in a relieved tone as he joined the Hardys in Officer Con Riley's office. Frank and Joe had just explained to Riley the specifics of the speedway incidents.

"No one here at police headquarters thought you were guilty of larceny," Con told Chet, "but the evidence meant we had to hold you."

"We're going to find out how this stolen stereo is related to the other problems out at the speedway," Joe told Con.

"I'm sure you can take care of it," Riley said as the three left the station.

"Tell us what happened from the beginning," Frank said to Chet as Joe drove away from police headquarters.

"The police woke me up around eight this morning," Chet said. "They pounded on the door until I let them in. Con Riley was holding a car stereo and asking me where I got it."

"What did you tell him?" Joe asked.

"I told him it wasn't mine."

"Then he asked me if it was my jeep that was in the driveway, and I told him yes," Chet continued. "He said he had found the radio in it." Chet shook his head. "I couldn't believe it."

"Where was the jeep parked?" Joe asked.

"In the driveway, right where it stalled."

"Con said specifically the stereo had been in the Saurion?" Frank asked.

"The anonymous caller said it was, so Con Riley talked to Felix Stock," Chet replied, "and Stock told him the serial number matched. He said the Saurion has custom-made stereos."

"Whoever made that call is probably behind the threats against Stock and Katie," Frank said.

"And the caller knows where the Saurion's hidden," Joe added. "Looks as if he wanted to frame Chet."

"Let's get out to the speedway and look around again," Frank said.

Joe headed the van north out of Bayport. Using the cellular phone, Frank put through a call to the speedway. Stock picked up the phone on the first ring.

"Have you found the Saurion?" Frank asked.

"No," Stock told him grimly. "And I don't see how we'll be able to finish one of the production cars in time for tomorrow's race. Too much work has to be performed by hand. And Marvin doesn't answer my calls," he added.

"Marvin Tarpley?" Frank asked, remembering the man's name from last evening's computer check.

"My mechanic," Stock told Frank.

"We'll solve this case," Frank said to Stock. "And we'll find that prototype." He hung up and told Joe and Chet what Stock had said.

"We'd better add Tarpley to our list of suspects," Joe said. "He was banned from the racing association. There might be a motive there."

"And I want to check on something strange I noticed yesterday at the speedway," Frank added. "Those strips of dead grass between the buildings. Why would grass burn out like that?"

"No sprinkler system?" Chet suggested.

"But the grass is green on both sides of the browned-out areas," Frank remarked.

Joe slowed the van as they approached the speedway entrance. He wrote Callie's name on the back of one of the demolition derby passes Curt Kiser had given Chet and left it at the pass gate.

"What a bunch of junkers," Chet said as Joe slowed the van so they could look at the preparations for the evening's demolition derby. "They look as if they've already been demolished."

Joe didn't see a model made less than fifteen years ago, and most were older. All of them were dented and rusty, but they were brightly painted.

Joe hit the brakes when a wiry young man in greasy jeans stepped out into the roadway and signaled for them to stop.

The man peered into the driver's window. "Is one of you the guy who's driving tonight?" he asked. "They're supposed to send someone right over to take a practice run. I'm in a bind since Tarpley left."

Joe immediately recognized the man. He was the tough guy's companion from the Circuit Diner. But the young man didn't seem to recognize Joe.

"What happened to Tarpley?" Joe asked.

"Who knows," the man said disgustedly. "He was bragging about making some *real* money."

Frank and Joe exchanged glances.

"So who's the driver?" the man wanted to know. "That guy there?" He pointed at Chet.

"Not me," Chet said, shaking his head. "No way."

"He's our manager," Joe said quickly. "I'm the one who drives. That is, I've driven racing cars."

"Park your van over there in the infield by that block building," the man said. He started to step back, then reached his hand through the window. "Name's Rusk," he said, "Dwaine Rusk. I'm managing tonight's derby." He peered at them. "It seems like I've seen you guys somewhere before."

63

"Frank and Joe Hardy," Joe said, shaking hands. "And that's Chet Morton."

"Are you nuts?" Chet whispered.

"Probably," Joe admitted. He turned the van toward the derby pit area and then stopped while he waited for a tow truck to pass. "But that's one of the men from the diner yesterday."

"It definitely is," Frank said, nodding. "I recognized him, too. And I have a feeling it was Marvin Tarpley he was having lunch with."

"These your new drivers, Dwaine?" a familiar voice asked. Joe turned to see that Curt Kiser was approaching, wearing his usual sunglasses.

Rusk nodded and shrugged. "The blond guy's driving," he told Kiser. "He seems pretty green, though."

"I can drive," Joe told Kiser calmly.

Kiser's eyes opened wide in surprise when he recognized Joe.

"We'll find out," Rusk said with a snort. "Start up that purple job over there, and I'll give you a little test."

Rusk was chuckling as Joe got out of the van and walked toward a heavily dented purple sedan.

"And get that van parked," Rusk ordered Frank.

"Was Joe bitten by the racing bug?" Curt Kiser asked as he slipped into the passenger side when Frank got behind the wheel.

"One of his fantasies is to drive in the Indianapolis five hundred," Frank told the speedway owner.

64

"The demolition derby is starting at the bottom," Kiser said, shaking his head. "But Rusk likes to challenge his drivers."

"Tell me about Dwaine Rusk," Frank said.

"Dwaine would like to drive in the Indy, too." Kiser chuckled. "But he's having too much fun running the derby."

"Is Marvin Tarpley a friend of his?" Frank asked.

"I wouldn't say that," Kiser replied. "Tarpley's one of those guys who's always bragging about some big deal. The last big deal he was involved in got him thrown out of auto racing."

Frank remembered the information about Tarpley on the computer. He was about to ask Kiser what the deal was when Chet tapped him on the shoulder.

"Hey, Joe got that ugly junker started." Chet pointed at the purple car with the large yellow letters reading Purple Machine.

Pulling into a space next to the wooden derby fence, Frank looked out into the arena where Joe was fishtailing the purple car.

"He handles it pretty well," Chet said.

"He'd better," Kiser said, "because here comes Rusk. I've seen Dwaine Rusk ram into a car at full speed, even when the driver in the other car lowered his flag."

"Lowered his flag?" Frank asked.

"You mean your brother doesn't know the rules?" Kiser asked. "See that little red flag right above the driver's window? Whenever a driver's in trouble, or wants to throw in the towel, he breaks off that flag. You never hit a car that's snapped off its flag.''

Handling the purple junker was a far cry from driving the Saurion, Joe realized, but the old car had some power. That allowed him to accelerate, then simultaneously hit the brakes and spin the steering wheel.

Joe was pulling out of a spin when he caught sight of a black and white zebra-striped car bearing down on him from the pits. With its grille gone, the car appeared to be leering at him.

Joe righted the Purple Machine, neatly dodging his zebra-striped opponent.

"Brace yourself, loser!" Rusk shouted at Joe as he roared past the Purple Machine.

Wrenching the wheel, Joe maneuvered into an angle toward the back end of the zebra-striped car. He floored the accelerator, and the Purple Machine glanced off the fender of the junker, smashing the taillight and popping the trunk lid. He saw an expression of rage come over Rusk's face when he looked over his shoulder at Joe.

The black and white car swung around and caught up with Joe. He had to admit that Rusk's car was faster. Rusk accelerated to full speed and smashed into the back of the Purple Machine.

Joe felt his breath knocked out of him. Without the shoulder harness he would have flown straight out the windshield. Clearing his head, Joe realized the engine had stalled. He turned the key and pumped the gas pedal. The grinding noise diverted his attention from the growing roar from Rusk's car.

Wham! The zebra-striped car hit Joe once more, knocking the Purple Machine sideways.

Joe turned the key again. This time the car didn't even grind. Joe decided he had better get out of the Purple Machine. He heard Rusk's car roaring straight toward him.

Joe struggled with the safety belt. It seemed to be jammed.

"Break off your flag!" Frank Hardy yelled across the arena at his brother. But Joe couldn't hear over the roar of the other car.

Frank sprinted out into the arena toward the Purple Machine. As he ran, he saw the black and white car crash broadside into Joe's car.

"Joe!" Frank cried. But Joe had disappeared from sight. In fact, the Purple Machine itself seemed to disappear. The last Frank saw of Joe's derby car, it was collapsing like an accordion file of purple metal.

7 Swallowed Up

Frank raced up to the wrecked purple car. He saw that the Purple Machine had rolled over on its side, and the roof had collapsed. "Joe!" he shouted hoarsely.

"He didn't break down his flag!" Dwaine Rusk said defensively as he climbed out of the zebra-striped car.

Frank peered inside the car. The driver's seat was completely flattened under the twisted roof supports.

"These old cars sure have roomy backseats," Frank suddenly heard his brother say.

"Joe, are you okay?"

"Of course I'm okay. Just help me out of here."

Frank wrenched the mangled driver's bucket seat

to the side. There was barely enough opening for Joe to wiggle through.

"Now, *that* was fun!" the younger Hardy insisted as Chet reached the wreck. "But I was afraid I wouldn't be able to slip out of that safety harness. I thought it was jammed. But then it just popped open." He took off his helmet and combed his hair with his fingers.

"It's not supposed to do that. A driver could get hurt," Rusk said. "The harness must be broken."

"How did you get into the backseat?" Chet asked.

"As quick as I could," Joe said with a grin. "I ripped off the harness and did a fast scramble."

"Do you realize almost every car you've been in in the past couple of days has crashed?" Chet asked his friend.

"You want to crash a few more cars," Dwaine Rusk told Joe, "you can drive in the derby tonight."

"So you can ram him again?" Frank demanded.

"It's all right," Joe assured his brother. "I wasn't hurt."

"Your brother's got guts," Rusk admitted.

"Thanks," Joe said, trying to look modest.

"Be here by six at the latest," Rusk told him.

"I know you think I'm crazy," Joe told Frank as they started back across the arena, "but maybe if I hang out with these guys, I'll learn more about Tarpley."

When they got back to the van, Jason Dain came

69

up to them in one of the speedway's golf carts. Curt Kiser was sitting next to him. Dain smiled at the Hardys and Chet. "Curt tells me you're taking up a new career. I guess the investigation isn't going too well."

"Any sign of the Saurion?" Joe asked, ignoring Dain's remarks.

"Maintenance workers searched the grounds thoroughly yesterday," Curt Kiser told them. "If that prototype were still here, they would have found it."

"If it doesn't turn up soon," Dain added, "and Stock and his group can't get another car ready, the speedway stands to lose a pile of money."

"Have you sold a lot of tickets to the race?" Frank asked.

"It's sold out," Kiser told them.

"We believe the car is still on the speedway grounds," Frank said. "You don't mind if we look around again, do you?"

"Not at all," Kiser said with a shrug. "Let's go, Jason." Dain turned the cart and headed in the direction of the main office.

Rusk walked up to them. "Don't forget, six o'clock," he told Joe.

Frank turned to Rusk. "Was that Marvin Tarpley you had lunch with yesterday at the diner?"

"That's where I saw you!" Rusk exclaimed. "Are you looking for Marvin?"

"That depends," Joe replied. "Did Tarpley mention how he was going to make that big money he was talking about?"

"He told me it's spying," Rusk said. "Industrial spying. He said he had the circuitry for this great new invention, and he was going to sell the plans to Miyagi Motors. He said it would make him rich. That's why he quit the derby. He thinks his days working grub jobs are over."

"You don't think he really had anything to sell?" Joe asked Rusk.

"I think he might know how Felix Stock's new PEST system works," Rusk said. "After all, he *is* Stock's mechanic."

"Did you know the Saurion prototype disappeared yesterday?" Frank asked.

"Sure," Rusk answered. "There were people over here searching the area."

Frank thanked Rusk, then turned to Joe and Chet. "We've got to find Tarpley, but first we have to find the car. I think we should split up and search again," he said. "We've missed something."

"Since it's lunchtime," Chet said, "I'll start my search at the lunch wagon parked by the office."

Frank and Joe started off in the direction of Gasoline Alley. "Here's that brown grass you're so interested in," Joe said as the brothers cut across the infield.

"Weird, isn't it?" Frank said slowly. "It's like someone drew lines. There's green grass on one side, brown grass on the other."

71

"Let's not worry about it now," Joe said. "I'll take the north half, you take the south. Besides the Saurion," he added, "we're looking for a machine that counterfeits license plates."

"And let's ask around for anyone whose hobby is remote-control cars," Frank added. "I'll meet you at Building A." Frank jogged off toward the south end of the racetrack, then systematically went about visiting every building.

An hour later Frank had still not made any progress. Scanning the speedway property, he started walking toward Building A. Suddenly he stopped.

"Wait a minute," he said to himself. "Where *are* they?"

"Where are what?" a nearby woman's voice asked.

Frank turned and found himself facing Katie Bratton. "The electric poles," Frank said. "They've got lights around the track, but where are all the wires? There aren't any power lines on the grounds."

"I don't know. I guess I never thought about it," Katie admitted.

"They must be underground," Frank murmured, answering his own question.

"It's too bad you haven't found the Saurion yet," she said sadly. "That race meant so much to Felix."

"The race means just as much to Takeo Ota,"

72

Frank told her pointedly. "By the way, Joe and I don't think he had anything to do with the Saurion's disappearance."

"Maybe it's someone else out at Miyagi Motors," she suggested.

"We were thinking more along the lines of someone right here at the speedway," Frank said.

"That's ridiculous," Katie insisted. "Who would want to harm Felix Stock?"

"How about Marvin Tarpley?" Frank said. "Do you have any idea where he is?"

"Hey," Katie said casually, "racetrack people are here one day, gone somewhere else the next." Katie shrugged and walked away.

"Did you find anything?" Joe asked his brother as he approached from the north end of the grounds.

"I didn't find the Saurion, if that's what you mean," Frank said. Before he could say more, Chet jogged over to the brothers.

"No Saurion," he said, breathing heavily, "but I did go all the way up to the top of the officials' tower, and from up there you can see those patches of dead grass running every which way."

"Is there a pattern?" Frank asked quickly.

"It's like they're in between the buildings," Chet replied. "Not all of the buildings, though. Just the older ones."

"That's it!" Frank snapped his fingers. "I think I know where the Saurion is hidden."

Frank broke into a run. Joe and Chet looked at

each other, exchanging a puzzled glance, and hurried after him.

"I thought you were nuts for driving that derby car," Chet told Joe, "but your brother's acting even crazier."

Rounding Building B, Frank headed for a ramshackle wooden shed attached to the end of the warehouse. Looking at the ground, he saw that the shack sat squarely in the middle of a strip of burned-out grass.

Joe saw his brother pull open the door and disappear inside the old shed. Suddenly he heard a loud crash and the sound of Frank crying out.

Joe sprinted into the shed. In the dim light he didn't see the gaping hole. "Help!" Joe yelled as he pitched forward and down into the black void.

8 Fire!

"Frank! Joe!" Chet cried as he looked down into the trapdoor set in the floor of the shed. "Are you down there?"

Joe heard Chet's voice dimly at first, then, as his head cleared, the voice seemed to grow louder.

"Are you all right?" he heard Chet call.

"Light," Joe said with a groan. "I need some light."

Joe sat up slowly, then climbed shakily to his feet. He tried to get his bearings and sort out what had happened while he waited for Chet to return.

"Frank!" he cried out suddenly, remembering why he had rushed into the shed in the first place. "Frank, are you down here?" Joe called, his voice echoing in the musty area.

"I'm letting down a flashlight on the end of this rope," Chet called from the shed above. "I've turned it on."

"Hurry," Joe said in a desperate tone. "I can't find Frank."

Moments later Joe saw the light dangling in the darkness. Joe untied the flashlight and aimed it at the area around him. He saw that he was in a narrow tunnel. Pipes wrapped in crumbling plaster insulation ran along the side walls. There were conduits and cables attached to the low ceiling.

Then he saw his brother. Frank was sprawled on the concrete floor behind him.

Joe knelt down next to Frank. With relief Joe found his brother's pulse and then slapped him on the face to rouse him. Frank moaned softly.

"I need a wet cloth down here!" Joe yelled up at Chet.

While Joe waited with his brother, Chet found an old stepladder and a rag. He soaked the cloth in water from a tap on the side of Building B, then hurried back to the shed. Nervously Chet lowered the ladder in the trapdoor opening. Then he climbed gingerly down into the darkness.

"I think he's going to be okay," Joe said. He applied the wet cloth to his brother's head. After a few moments Frank opened his eyes.

"The last thing I remember," Frank groaned, "is falling."

"You hit," Joe told him. "Hard."

"You're telling me," his brother said, rubbing the lump on his head. "But the good news is, I was right. Do you know where we are?"

"A hole in the ground?" Chet asked.

"We're in an extensive tunnel system," Frank said. "I knew there was some explanation for those patches of brown grass."

"I don't get it," Chet said.

"Cement is porous," Frank explained. "These tunnels absorb the groundwater that would keep the grass green, like it is on both sides of the tunnels."

"These tunnels are used for heating and electrical systems," Joe said.

"And you think the Saurion's down here in this tunnel," Chet concluded.

"While we search for the car," Frank said, turning to Chet, "we'd like you to find Callie in case we're not out of here in time to meet her. And while you're at it, maybe you could drive the van back over to that food truck and get us something to eat. I'm feeling a little wobbly."

"I can do that," Chet said as he began climbing up the ladder.

"Let's plan on meeting at Building A by five o'clock," Frank said. "Then Joe can get over to the demolition derby."

Leading the way, Joe began walking deeper into

77

the dank tunnel. The floor was rough and unfinished. The walls, he noticed, were made of concrete, like the floor.

"So far all we've seen is rubbish and a couple of rats," Joe said several minutes later.

Frank nodded. "Except for some of the pipes turning upward, there's no sign of any connection with Building A above. No door, not even a hatch."

"Then let's go back the other way."

"Not just yet," Frank said. "Let's say whoever took the Saurion pushed it out the front door of Building A, then rolled it away from Felix Stock's compound."

Suddenly Joe stopped. "There's a back overhead door in Building A!" he exclaimed.

"That's true," Frank said, "but it's behind a pile of crates."

"Doesn't matter," Joe insisted. "That's how the car disappeared. It was pushed out the back door."

Abruptly the tunnel turned to the left.

"There's something up ahead," Frank noted as the flashlight beam shone on a barrier.

"It's a wooden wall and a door," Joe said.

"And it looks relatively new," Frank commented.

Joe jiggled the latch, but the door wouldn't open. "It's locked," he said in a disappointed tone.

Removing a small knife from his pocket, Frank worked the latch. "Forget it," he said finally. "There's a hasp and a padlock on the other side."

78

"Maybe I can break the door down," Joe said. He threw his shoulder against the door, but it held. He tried it again, but it still wouldn't budge.

"We need to hit it together," Frank said.

On a count of three the Hardys used all their strength to ram the door. This time Joe went sprawling as the latch on the other side sprang free and the heavy door swung in on a large underground room.

Frank helped Joe to his feet, then shined the flashlight around the room. Joe switched on a hanging lightbulb and found himself staring at a canvas-covered automobile. "It's the Saurion!" Joe cried. "We found it."

The Hardys pulled the heavy canvas cover off the sleek red sports car.

"There's the hole in the dashboard, where the stereo goes," Frank said, pointing.

"Nothing else seems to be missing," Joe said as he examined the Saurion. "The odometer doesn't even show a mile since I dropped the transmission."

He got down on his back and looked under the sports car with the flashlight. "The transmission's still got those blown seals," he reported. "We've got to tell Felix Stock we found his car."

"It looks like someone was working on the brakes over here," Frank said. "There's grease all over."

"Any fingerprints?" Joe asked right away.

"Maybe, but they're smeared."

"Then to be safe, I'll simply have to wipe them off," came a cold voice from the corner behind them.

Frank whirled around, and Joe slipped hurriedly out from under the car.

"Freeze!" the voice commanded. "I have a gun."

In the dim light of the single bulb Frank saw that the man was wearing a racing suit, a black racing helmet, and a dark visor that hid his eyes. He was short and looked muscular.

"That's a flare gun," Frank pointed out.

"You think it's a toy, you're welcome to try me." The man in black aimed it at Frank's head. "Now, get away from the car!" the man ordered.

Frank backed up carefully, followed by Joe.

"I regret that I am going to have to do away with you two. The others won't be happy, but I don't see any other way."

"Let's look at our options," Joe suggested, trying to gain some time.

"You don't have any," the man said coldly. "Take this rope," he added, tossing a coil of rope to Joe. "Tie your brother's hands and feet to that pipe over by the workbench wall. Now!" he snarled.

Frank backed up to the pipe, and Joe tied up his brother.

The man with the gun went over and looked at the knots. "Nice work," he said to Joe.

Joe remained silent.

"You come over here," the man continued, "and turn around."

As Joe did as he was told, Frank watched the man suddenly hit his brother on the back of the head. Joe fell to the floor, unconscious.

"Hey!" Frank shouted.

The man in black laughed.

While Frank began working at the knots binding his hands, he saw their assailant take a pile of oily rags from a workbench. He threw them under the bench, then dragged some cardboard boxes and several wooden crates over. Taking a can of high-octane additive, he emptied it on the pile.

"It's damp down here," the man said. "Wouldn't a nice warm fire feel good?" He laughed menacingly.

Frank watched as the man raised the flare gun and aimed it at the pile of debris. The helmeted man pulled the trigger.

The sudden burst of brilliant white magnesium fire blinded Frank. Immediately he could feel the heat as the flare ignited the combustible liquid.

"Too bad it had to end this way," the man said as he hurried off down one of the tunnels.

"Joe!" Frank called. "Can you hear me?"

But Joe was still out cold. And as smoke began to fill the basement room, Frank found it was hard to even see his brother. Frank's eyes began to water, and the smoke in the air made it difficult to breathe. "Joe!" he tried again.

We've got to get out of this, Frank said to himself. He was growing dizzy from lack of oxygen. His head drooped forward, and he knew he was only seconds away from passing out.

9 Where's Callie?

Frank made a superhuman effort to stay conscious. Although Joe had tied him up, Frank knew his brother was experienced at tying slipknots.

Frank struggled with the ropes. Soon he managed to work loose his wrists and untie the ropes around his ankles. Grabbing the fire extinguisher from a nearby wall, Frank immediately smothered the flames.

He knelt down next to his brother, who was still unconscious. "Come on," Frank said, slapping Joe's face.

Slowly Joe came to. "Did you catch him?" he asked groggily.

"He got away," Frank said. "But we've still got the Saurion."

"How do we get out of here?" Joe said as Frank helped him to his feet.

"We go out the same way the Saurion came in," Frank told him.

The Hardys headed back out of the large basement room into the tunnel through which the helmeted man had fled. Joe shone the flashlight on the tire tracks that cut through the dust of the concrete floor.

"There's no question that this is the way the Saurion was brought into that room," Frank said.

"There's a ramp," Joe said when he saw the tunnel divide. One branch headed off to the left, the other sloped upward. Joe started up the ramp.

"These are just boards thrown over the opening from outside," Joe said. Pushing a board aside, he found himself looking out into the late-afternoon light. He hoisted himself up. His brother followed.

"We're behind Building A," Joe said. "There's the overhead door we thought couldn't be used."

Frank looked around. "And this old tunnel ramp is shielded by these oil drums."

"Let's get over to Building A," Joe said. "Stock should have a small tractor or something to help us bring up the Saurion."

"Got any ideas on who the guy in the black helmet was?" Frank asked his brother as they headed over to the Stock Motor Car Company.

"Maybe it was Marvin Tarpley," Joe said.

"The guy had the same build—short and muscular," Frank said. "Anyway, at least now we know that because of where the Saurion was hidden, the thief and the person who's responsible for the incident is probably someone right on the grounds."

"But who has something to gain from hiding only the Saurion?" Joe asked. "And who would want to go so far as to try and *kill* people over the car?"

"That's what we've got to find out," Frank said. "Right now," he added, looking at his watch, "we've got to tell Felix Stock his prototype's been found. Then you've got a new job with the derby."

Frank saw Chet sitting in the van when the brothers reached the front of Building A.

"Hey, I thought you guys would never get here," Chet said as they approached. "I almost ate all this food myself." Through the van window he handed the Hardys a cardboard tray piled with hot dogs, bags of chips, and soda.

"Did you see Callie over there?" Frank asked as he unwrapped a hot dog.

"No, but I overheard Dwaine Rusk complain that Joe's late."

"Where's Felix Stock?" Joe asked, munching on a potato chip.

"He's working on a second Saurion," Chet said. "But he says he'll never be ready in time for tomorrow night."

"Oh, yes, he will," Joe said. He bit into his hot dog, then turned and entered the building. Joe was smiling when he entered Building A. He found

Felix Stock going over some paperwork at his desk, and Joe thought he looked pretty glum.

"Your prototype is parked in a tunnel under these buildings," Joe said, getting right to the point.

Stock stared at him for a moment as if he couldn't believe what he was hearing. "You *found* it?" he said finally. "But how . . . where?"

"It's a long story," Frank said, coming up behind Joe. Hurriedly Frank told the engineer about the helmeted man and where the prototype was hidden.

Joe dodged out of the way as a now-smiling Felix Stock raced outside. The Hardys hurried after the engineer.

A few moments later Stock was standing in the basement room gazing at the Saurion, a happy expression on his face. "Thanks, guys," he said warmly, turning to Frank and Joe. "You really came through for me."

When they got back up to the ground, Frank attached chains to the tractor that would pull the Saurion out of the tunnel.

"It'll take all night," Stock said, sitting at the wheel of the tractor, "but I'll have the prototype ready for that race."

"I've got to get to the derby," Joe said.

"Good luck," Frank said. His brother waved and jogged toward the derby's infield compound.

Frank glanced at his watch again. Callie was probably here by now, he thought. He and Chet turned their attention to helping Stock pull the Saurion out of the underground tunnel and up the ramp. Fifteen minutes later Stock was raising the Saurion upon a hydraulic lift in Building A.

"Why did you decide to build the Saurion here?" Frank asked Stock.

"I might be a fairly good engineer," Stock explained, "but I put all my money into designing the car itself. I did a lot of research and hired consultants. When it came time to actually build one, there wasn't much money left. Curt offered to let me use his property here in return for a share of any profits the Saurion earns."

"No money went to Curt up front?" Frank asked.

"Not a cent. Like I said, I couldn't have done that anyway," Stock went on. "Every dime I've got is in the PEST system. Even if the Saurion doesn't sell, I think the PEST technology could be worth a few bucks." He smiled, then whispered confidentially, "And I'm the only one who knows the secret circuitry!"

"What about Marvin Tarpley?" Frank asked. "Dwaine Rusk told me Tarpley knows the circuitry."

"Yeah," Stock said, "Tarpley may have figured it out, but he'd have no means to apply it. He'd need a financial backer if he wanted to use my design."

"Do you think Tarpley would try to sell the design?"

"Well, I guess I never thought about that," Stock said, frowning.

"Where is Tarpley, anyway?" Frank asked.

"I heard he quit the derby," Stock said, "and he hasn't showed up around here in a few days. If he doesn't get in touch with me soon, I'm afraid he's out of a job."

"Does Tarpley have any contractual rights to the Saurion?" Frank asked.

"Nope, only Kiser," Stock replied.

"Does Kiser stand to make money only from the car or from the PEST system, too?"

"I told Curt the deal was for the Saurion only," Felix Stock replied evenly.

"But isn't the PEST system an integral part of the car?" Frank wanted to know.

"You sound just like those lawyers," Felix Stock said, frowning. "I say it isn't, but one lawyer I talked to claims it's standard equipment."

"I'd like to look over the contract with Kiser," Frank said. "Criminal motives are often hidden in fine print."

"I'll see if I can find it later," Stock said. "I know I need a business manager, like Kiser's got Jason Dain. But I keep putting it off."

"Is that Jason Dain's job here?" Frank asked. "He's Curt Kiser's business manager?"

"He's Curt Kiser's partner," Katie Bratton interrupted. She was standing a few feet away from Frank, holding an envelope. "Jason Dain is a man of many talents. He's an accountant who also knows a lot about cars. If anyone can turn this track into a money-maker, Dain can. And—" Suddenly her eyes grew wide. "You found it!" she cried out, hurrying over to the car. "I can't believe it. Where was it?"

Frank wanted to keep as many details about the case as secret as possible, so he quickly replied, "All the facts aren't in yet, but we'll let you know. . . ." Noticing the envelope in Katie's hand, he changed the subject. "Is that a message for someone?"

Katie paused, then held out the envelope to Frank. "Jason gave this to me when I left his office. He said it was delivered less than an hour ago."

Frank saw his name written on the front when he took the envelope. He opened it and unfolded the paper inside. Curiosity turned quickly to fear as he read the handwritten letter.

"Is something wrong?" Katie asked, seeing the worried expression on Frank's face.

Frank looked up from the paper. "This is a note from my girlfriend, Callie Shaw," he said. "It says she's been held up and won't be able to meet me here for the demolition derby."

"I'm sure she has a good reason," Katie said.

"The problem is," Frank said tensely, "this is not Callie's handwriting."

10 Going for a Ride

"When did Jason Dain give you this letter?" Frank urgently asked Katie Bratton.

"Just a few minutes ago," she said. "He knew I was coming over here."

"How did he know that?" Chet asked suspiciously.

"Because I *told* him!" Katie said hotly. "Look, I know things have been crazy around here for the past few days, but we aren't going to accomplish anything if we accuse each other of being part of some plot."

"I'm sorry," Chet said sheepishly.

"It's okay," Katie said with a nod. "I hope your girlfriend's all right, Frank. You guys do what you have to do, and I'll help Felix get the Saurion ready."

Frank signaled to Chet to follow him out of the building. "We've got to find Callie," Frank said grimly.

"What do you think happened to her?" Chet asked. "Do you think she's in danger?"

"It doesn't look good," Frank replied. "Someone is probably holding Callie for some reason. We've got to start searching."

"Where do we start?" Chet asked.

"First we need to check out this letter," Frank said. He hurried to the van and removed the fingerprinting kit and a high-power microscope.

Frank turned on a bright incandescent lamp inside the van and held the letter up to the light. "Twenty-pound bond," he said. "This paper's available in any office supply store."

Frank dusted both the paper and the envelope lightly with a fine black powder. Then he blew the excess from the surfaces. He was able to see a few whorls of what looked like a print. "I think it's a thumbprint," he said. "Hand me the camera, please."

Chet got the camera from the back of the van and handed it to Frank, who fitted it with a macro lens. Then, holding the camera very still, he snapped an electronic picture of the print.

"Is this the gadget that lets you take a picture you

can see on your computer screen?" Chet wanted to know.

"You got it," Frank said. "What we do now is transfer the signals from the digital disk into our laptop fax machine, then send it through the modem to Con Riley, so he can run a check."

"Pretty slick," Chet said.

After sending the fingerprint to the Bayport police, Frank called Miyagi Motors to find out what time Callie had left.

"Four-thirty," Frank said after talking with Takeo Ota for a few minutes and hanging up. "She's nearly an hour and a half late. Mr. Ota also told me they found a glitch in the software controlling the robot arm that hit me."

"Does that take Miyagi Motors off the list of suspects?" Chet wanted to know.

"More than likely," Frank answered in a distracted tone. "We'd better drive the van over to the front gate. It's too far to walk, and I don't want to waste any time."

When they reached the ticket taker's window, Frank parked in the closest spot and hurried out of the van.

"I'm looking for a young woman named Callie Shaw," Frank told the ticket taker, holding open his wallet so the man could see Callie's picture. "What I need to know is, did she claim a ticket?"

"Well, a lot of people have been coming through," the ticket taker said, scratching his head.

"Could you just look at this photo and tell me if you saw this woman claim a ticket here?" Frank said, trying not to sound impatient.

"I'm sorry," the ticket taker said, squinting at the photo, "but I've only been on duty for a few minutes, and I don't remember anyone matching that specific description or anyone with the name Callie."

"Thanks," Frank told him. "We don't know any more now than we did before," he added gloomily as he and Chet moved away from the ticket office.

"We're going to miss Joe's derby," Chet said.

"Wait a minute," Frank said, stopping short. "The man at the gate said he'd only been on duty a few minutes."

"So what?" Chet said in a puzzled tone.

"He just came on duty," Frank said. "That means someone else was there when Callie might have picked up her ticket. We've got to talk with that man again." Frank hurried back to the pass gate.

The ticket taker looked irritated. "I told you, I didn't see your friend."

"You said you'd only been on duty here a few minutes," Frank said. "That means there was someone here before you. Who was it?"

"Okay, okay," the man said. "For all I know your friend came in before I got here."

"Who was on this gate before you?" Frank demanded.

"It was a guy named Marvin Tarpley. He works

93

for Stock and for the demolition derby, but I'd heard he quit. Anyway," the ticket taker continued, "that's who was taking tickets when I returned from the office."

"Why did you go to the office?" Frank asked.

"They said they'd lost my Social Security number. They needed it for my payroll records."

"Who did you talk to?"

"Mr. Dain."

Frank thanked the man and turned to Chet. "Marvin Tarpley's on the grounds somewhere," Frank said grimly. "And I'll bet you he's got Callie. And I think Jason Dain is in on whatever this scheme is."

"What do we do?" Chet asked.

"Tarpley's home turf is the demolition derby," Frank said. "So let's leave the van here and walk over to that area." Frank and Chet began threading their way through the crowd still making their way to the grandstand.

"If Tarpley's done anything to Callie," Frank said evenly, "I'll make sure he spends the rest of his life in prison."

"We'll find her," Chet said reassuringly.

Frank heard the loudspeaker overhead welcome the crowd to the big demolition derby. People cheered over the roar of the engines.

The derby pits were indistinguishable from the rest of the round dirt arena. Frank counted eight brightly colored junkers. Their drivers and mechanics were tinkering with the engines.

"I thought you guys were going to miss the start," Joe said, sprinting over to Frank and Chet.

"I think that Callie's been kidnapped," he told his brother in a low voice, then filled him in on the details.

"Last call for the first race," the voice on the loudspeaker announced.

"That's me," Joe said. "Do you want me to bag the race and help you find Callie?"

"Go ahead and race," Frank told him. "Chet and I will look for Tarpley."

"Come on, rookie, let's go!" Dwaine Rusk shouted as he came running up to Joe. "You want to wreck a few junkers or not?"

"I'm ready," Joe told him.

"I've got you in the sweetest little candy apple red bomb you ever saw," Rusk went on. "That's why it's called the Red Bomb." He chuckled, then added, "And it's got four hundred horses."

Joe ran off toward the arena where the cars were lined up facing the grandstand. As Rusk turned to leave, Frank said, "I hear your good buddy Tarpley is back."

"He isn't my buddy," Rusk insisted.

"Have you seen him here?"

"Sure," Rusk said. "After all, he's a good mechanic. When I told him your brother was going to drive the Red Bomb, he insisted on setting it up for him. He even put the weights in the trunk."

"Weights?" Frank asked.

"Yeah, we put cement blocks and stuff in the trunk to give the cars more stability," Rusk explained. "One reason the Purple Machine rolled over so easily this morning was because it wasn't weighted."

"Where's Marvin Tarpley now?" Frank asked.

"He could be anywhere. He wants to drive in the derby once more for old time's sake." Rusk started to leave, then turned back to Frank and added, "He's in the last round."

"One more question," Frank said. "I'm looking for a young woman." Frank showed him the picture of Callie. "She was supposed to meet me here tonight, and I have reason to believe she came in when Marvin Tarpley was working the pass gate."

"Could be," Rusk said with a shrug. "But I haven't seen her." Without giving Frank the chance to ask any more questions, Rusk headed for the pit area.

Frank glanced out into the arena and saw that Joe, helmet and goggles in place, was revving up the Red Bomb's engine. The starter dropped his flags. According to tradition, the cars backed away from the line, then began ramming into each other.

Frank watched the mayhem for a few moments, saw that Joe was doing well, then turned to scan the crowd in the stands. He didn't spot Marvin Tarpley.

He looked over at the infield and drew his breath in sharply. Marvin Tarpley was lounging at the corner of a garage.

Frank rounded the grandstand and hurried over to Tarpley.

"Marvin Tarpley?" Frank asked. The man turned. Frank thought Tarpley was surprised to see him.

"Did this young woman come through the pass gate earlier tonight while you were on duty here?" Frank held up Callie's picture.

Tarpley looked at the picture, then at Frank. "I don't think that's any of your business," he said, and turned back to watch the derby.

"I think it is," Frank said quietly, grabbing Tarpley's left arm and wrenching it behind his back. "Now, let's have an answer. Did you see her, yes or no?"

Tarpley winced. "Yes," he hissed.

"Did you let her in?" Frank continued.

"She's in, all right," Tarpley said as he writhed in Frank's grasp. He tried to chop down on Frank's forearm, but Frank twisted Tarpley's arm higher up his back.

"Right now," Tarpley gasped, "your precious girlfriend's taking a ride, and you better hope that

97

hotshot brother of yours avoids rear-end colli-sions."

"What are you talking about?" Frank demanded.

"We ran out of cement blocks for weight," Tarpley said, sneering, "so I threw her in the trunk instead. Right this very minute your girlfriend's in the demolition derby."

11 Over the Edge

Frank was momentarily gripped by shock. He couldn't believe that Callie was locked in the trunk of Joe's demolition derby junker.

In hesitating, Frank gave Marvin Tarpley the opening he wanted. Tarpley pulled free and took off.

"I've got to get Callie out of there!" Frank exclaimed, turning toward the derby arena. The deafening sound of crunching metal told Frank that he had no time to waste.

Frank had counted eight cars at the start to the derby. Surveying the wreckage strewn around the arena, he saw that Joe's Red Bomb was one of only three remaining junkers. The winner, he knew, was the last car that could still be driven.

Meanwhile, in the arena, Joe was impressed that the Red Bomb's engine was still running. But he had taken a bad hit in his right front wheel. He felt the old car pull to the right and figured the axle was badly bent.

"Don't fall apart on me now," Joe told the car. He slammed it into reverse. Wheels spinning, he shot out of the path of a faded green sedan. The green car grazed Joe's front fender. Joe felt the jolt. He knew that if he were not securely held in his seat by the safety harness, he might be thrown against the door and window frames or the metal dashboard.

And whatever it was that was rolling around loose back in his trunk, he thought to himself, was going to be reduced to powder by the time the race was over.

Seeing an opportunity to nail the green car, Joe shifted his car into drive and floored it. He rocketed forward, the green car in his sights. The Red Bomb crashed full speed into the green car's front fender.

The green car stalled. Joe smiled with satisfaction when he saw steam rise from its punctured radiator.

"One to go," he said to himself. He shifted into reverse. Then his eyes widened in alarm as he saw Frank hop over the fence into the arena. Frank was waving frantically. Seeing his brother made Joe hesitate. He saw his last rival, a battered orange sedan. It was coming from the far side of the arena.

100

"Break off your flag!" Frank yelled.

Joe's goggles were splattered with mud and oil, but he took them off instinctively, as if they were somehow keeping him from hearing Frank.

"Break your flag!" Frank shouted again, pointing toward the roof of the Red Bomb.

Joe couldn't make out what Frank was saying, but it was clear something was wrong. And a quick glance in the other direction showed him he was seconds from being rear-ended.

Joe reached up and snapped off the red flag. The orange car veered off at the last moment. There was wild cheering from the grandstand as the winner began his victory lap.

"Joe!" Frank cried as he ran up to the Red Bomb. "Callie's in the trunk!"

Joe immediately pushed the automatic trunk release button. Nothing happened. "It's jammed!" Joe exclaimed as he jumped out of the car.

Dwaine Rusk came running out into the arena. "What's going on out here?" he shouted at Joe.

"There's a woman in the trunk of this car," Frank said. "Callie!" he shouted at the trunk. There was no answer.

"Get a crowbar." Frank gestured frantically to Chet, who had been watching from the sidelines. Chet grabbed a tire iron from the pit and ran into the arena.

Frank rapped the trunk lid a couple of times with the crowbar. Suddenly the lid popped open. The

101

cheering crowd suddenly fell silent as they watched what was taking place in the arena.

Callie lay on an old carpet. Her eyes were blindfolded, and her face and arms were scratched and covered with dust. Her hands and legs were tied.

"Callie, I'll get you out of here as soon as possible."

Frank removed the adhesive-tape gag from her mouth and the blindfold. "Are you all right?" Frank asked anxiously, as he began untying the ropes.

"When you invited me to the demolition derby," she said dryly, pushing her hair out of her face, "I never thought *I* was going to be demolished."

While Frank helped her out of the trunk, Callie explained how the ticket taker had told her he had been instructed to escort her to the main office.

"As soon as we were inside the office," Callie continued, "someone clamped his hand over my mouth from behind, and the ticket taker tied me up."

"Marvin Tarpley," Frank said grimly.

"Did you see the other person?" Joe asked Callie.

"I tried, but they had me gagged and blindfolded before I had the chance," she answered.

"How about voices?" Frank asked. "Did they talk to each other?"

"All I heard was 'We warned the Hardys, and now they're going to pay,'" Callie said.

"This is awful," Dwaine Rusk said nervously. "I

102

mean, we run a reputable business around here. Callie could have been seriously injured."

"It's not your fault," Frank told the derby manager. "And we'll get Tarpley soon enough."

"I'll bring the van over," Chet said.

Frank gave Chet the keys and told him to meet the group at the front gate.

"It didn't mean anything at the time," Callie told Frank as they left the arena, "but I saw Tarpley over at Miyagi Motors early this morning."

"You're sure?" Frank asked. "Do you know what he was there for?"

"I heard him say Takeo Ota was expecting him," Callie replied. "The receptionist said there was a misunderstanding, because Tarpley didn't have an appointment."

"Maybe Joe and I were too hasty when we ruled out Miyagi Motors," Frank said thoughtfully.

"Tarpley was pretty insistent. He told the receptionist that he'd be back," Callie said.

"Since Callie was kidnapped right in the speedway's front office," Frank said to Joe, "that's the place to check before the staff reports for work tomorrow morning."

"We've got more problems," Chet told them when the Hardys and Callie reached the gate. "Someone punctured holes in all four tires on the van."

"And I think I know who did it," Frank said with a sigh.

Just then, Joe spotted Jason Dain in his golf cart. Joe waved him over.

"Something wrong?" Jason Dain asked as he pulled to a stop.

"Our tires were slashed," Joe said angrily.

"That's too bad," Dain said, glancing at the tires. "I'll tell Curt about this."

"Do you think you could loan us a speedway truck?" Chet asked.

Dain shook his head. "Sorry, guys," he said. "The only thing we've got is that white panel truck over there, and our insurance won't permit anyone but a speedway employee to drive it."

"Dain," Frank said, trying to hold his temper, "what do you know about the letter Katie delivered to me today? She said she got it from you."

"Yeah, I found it in my desk, so I asked her to give it to you," Dain said. "Why do you ask?"

Frank ignored the question and, instead, posed one of his own. "Why did you switch the ticket takers before the demo derby when Callie was due to pick up her ticket?"

"I don't know anything about her ticket, but I do know that I'm trying to run a business and that's no business of yours," Dain retorted. Before Frank could press him for further information, Dain sped off on his cart.

"Well, so much for the direct approach," Frank muttered. As he glanced over at the panel truck, his attention was caught by a striking gun metal gray sports car darting around the speedway access road toward them. It screeched to a halt.

"Which do you like better, the red or the silver?" Felix Stock asked proudly as he got out of the Saurion. "This is the one we were trying to prepare for the race before you found the prototype." Stock looked at Frank and Joe. "You guys don't look so happy."

"Somebody slashed our tires," Joe told him.

"That's terrible," Felix said. "I can't believe it. If you need a car, you can use this." Stock pointed toward the Saurion.

"Wow!" Chet gasped.

"You sure you don't mind?" Frank asked, his face lighting up.

"Go ahead and drive it," Stock insisted with a smile. "It's the least I can do after you recovered the prototype. Which, I am pleased to say, is nearly ready for the race. I'll be here all night working," Stock said. "If you can decide who gets to ride in the Saurion, the other two can use my sedan." Felix Stock called Katie Bratton on his walkie-talkie and asked her to bring his sedan over to the main entrance.

While they waited, Frank filled Felix in on the latest details of the case and told him of their plans to investigate the offices in the morning.

"Since I drove the prototype yesterday," Joe told Frank when the sedan arrived, "you and Callie go on ahead and drive this Saurion home."

105

Callie smiled. "I don't see any point in arguing with Joe," she said to Frank. "Do you?"

"We're on our way," Frank said excitedly. Frank got in and started the powerful V-8 engine, and its growl vibrated smoothly throughout the car. Callie sat in the passenger side.

"The sun is setting, so use your remote to lock the PEST system for night driving," Felix Stock told Frank.

Frank flicked on the locking switch. Then, shifting into first gear, he eased out the clutch.

"This car is incredible," Callie said in an awed tone as the Saurion shot forward through the speedway gate.

"When Joe drove the prototype yesterday," Frank said as they cruised down the road, "he said it was almost impossible to drive it slowly."

"He was on a racetrack," Callie reminded Frank. "But we're on Shore Road."

"This thing is great!" Frank exclaimed. "Here, let me pull over, and you can drive it on into town."

"If you insist," Callie said with an eager grin.

Knowing the handling was responsive to the touch, Frank turned the wheel a notch. He wanted to stop and watch the sunset from high above Barmet Bay, to their left.

Suddenly Callie gasped. "Everything's getting black!"

Frank saw that Callie was right. Only a moment before, he'd had a clear view of the pull-off. But the windshield was darkening rapidly. He could make out the faint light of a buoy far out in the bay, but that was all.

"Brace yourself!" Frank told Callie as he slammed on the brakes.

The driver's side front wheel hit one of the stout wooden posts supporting the low guardrail along the rim of the cliff. Frank twisted the wheel back toward the road. He couldn't see the guardrail through the darkened windshield, but he could feel the front of the Saurion rise up along the rail.

Callie screamed when she heard metal rip into the underside of the car.

Frank knew by the feel of the steering that the front end was off the ground. He continued to try steering the car, but he couldn't see a thing out the blackened windshield. He felt as if he were driving with his eyes closed.

"Frank!" Callie yelled. "Stop us before we go over the cliff!"

12 Breaking and Entering

Frank acted quickly. Grasping the emergency brake, he wrenched it up sharply. He and Callie were thrown violently forward against their seat belts, but the emergency brake held. Frank felt the engine stall, and the Saurion stopped.

"You okay?" Frank asked breathlessly.

"Yeah," she replied. "Just scared."

Frank tried unsuccessfully to open the driver's side door. Through the narrow crack he could see Barmet Bay a hundred feet straight down. "We've got to crawl out your side," Frank told Callie. "My door's right up against the guardrail."

As Frank followed Callie out of the car, he glanced at Shore Road and saw a white panel truck pass slowly by. When the driver saw Frank looking at him, he sped on past.

"We were being followed," Frank said. "It looked like the truck that attacked Chet's jeep. And the driver was wearing a racing helmet that hid his face."

Chet and Joe pulled up in Stock's sedan. "What happened this time?" Chet called from the sedan. He peered out at the Saurion.

Frank explained about the PEST system malfunctioning and then asked, "Did you see a white panel truck in front of you?"

"No, it must have been too far ahead," Joe said.

"It wouldn't surprise me if Tarpley was driving," Frank said. "I noticed that when we asked Dain if we could use one of the speedway's trucks, he mentioned a white panel truck."

Chet spoke up. "That means Dain's definitely mixed up in this."

"But what would he have to gain from sabotaging the Saurion?" Joe asked.

"Someone definitely sabotaged it," Callie pointed out, "or else Stock's high-tech window system is a joke."

"We'll look into it tomorrow," Frank said.

"What about the Saurion?" Callie asked. "We can't just leave it parked out here."

"We'd better push it away from the cliff," Joe said.

When the car was a safe distance away from the cliff, Frank reached across the passenger seat and found the remote on the floor under the brake pedal. He pressed the Start button, and the engine roared to life.

"Sounds good," Joe said. "But you can't drive it with the windows blacked out."

Switching the PEST lock to the On mode, Frank operated the adjustment button. "It's working now," he said as the glass areas lighted up.

"How could the system just fix itself like that?" Chet asked, puzzled.

"Good question," Frank said thoughtfully. "But there are a lot of questions that need answering before I'll believe this was a technical glitch."

He and Callie got back into the Saurion. Callie drove to her house. After saying good night, Frank and Joe took the Saurion, and Chet went home in the sedan.

The next morning Frank and Joe got up before Aunt Gertrude, grabbed some juice and toast, and headed out of the house.

After looking over the gray Saurion in the early morning light, Joe decided that aside from several scrapes, the car had been only moderately damaged in the near disaster at the cliffs. He took the wheel and backed the car out of the garage.

"People will start arriving at the speedway

around eight," Frank said as they roared off. "That gives us an hour and a half to turn up something."

Ten minutes later Joe pulled in to the main parking lot outside the speedway fence. He parked the Saurion behind a group of dumpsters in the corner of the lot. Then Frank led them along the twelve-foot-high chain-link fence until they reached a fairly secluded area hidden by trees and bushes. Frank gave Joe a boost in scaling the fence, then followed him over the top.

"The offices look empty," Frank said as they approached the concrete building. Except for a gold car, the small parking lot was vacant, and he could see no lights in the office windows.

Joe used an old parking garage key card to trip the latch on the speedway office. "You take Dain's office, I'll check Kiser's."

When Frank reached Dain's office, he found it was unlocked. Dain's desktop was bare, and hurriedly Frank went through the drawers. In the bottom drawer, under some quarterly reports, he found a remote-control device. Next to it was a box used to ship an automobile radar detector. Except for a circuit board, the box was empty. Frank studied the items and put them back.

Looking toward the far wall, Frank saw a bookcase. Most of the books were about accounting and auto racing, but two books, however, caught his eye. One was a book on electronic miniaturization. The other, called *Applications of Industrial Demolition,* was about explosives.

"Look at this!" Joe exclaimed as he entered Dain's office. He handed Frank a power card. Frank saw that it was smaller than the model he had found in Building C, but otherwise it looked the same.

"Kiser's got a closet full of remote-control stuff," Joe added.

Then Frank showed Joe the remote-control device and the book on explosives.

"What do you make of it?" Joe asked.

"I'm not sure yet," Frank admitted. "Let's take a look in Dain's closet," Frank suggested, walking over to the closet door. When he found it was locked, he used Joe's key card to open it. Looking into the closet, he found jackets and racing suits hanging on the coatrack.

"From what you said about Kiser's office, he's the one with the remote-control car hobby," Frank said, "but we're finding evidence in here linking Dain as well."

"Shh," Joe said suddenly. He heard the front door open, then close again. Somebody had just entered the lobby.

Frank slipped noiselessly behind a four-drawer file on the other side of the closet, and Joe hurried into the closet, switching off the light and easing the door closed.

Rubber-soled shoes, Frank thought when he was unable to hear footsteps. Then he heard the door of

Dain's office open. Someone pulled out one of the desk drawers and rummaged around.

Joe desperately wanted to get a look at the person. He reached out to open the door a crack. At that moment the closet door swung open.

Joe flattened himself against the back of the closet behind the racing suits. He was afraid that his rapidly pounding heart would give him away. He heard the sound of wire hangers on the rod.

Cautiously Joe peeked through the suits. The person suddenly stepped away and walked out of the office, closing the door behind him.

Joe bent over, picked up a piece of material that had fallen on the closet floor, and stuffed it in his pocket. Then he stayed frozen in place for a moment. "Let's wait a minute to be sure," Joe called softly, stepping out of the closet.

"That was close," Frank whispered as he slipped out from behind the file cabinets.

"But worth it, I think," Joe said excitedly. "I saw—"

"What did you see?" came a new voice from a dark corner of the room.

Frank stiffened as the fluorescent lights came on. Too late, he realized that *two* people had entered the speedway office, and only one had left.

Now the Hardys found themselves face to face with Marvin Tarpley.

"What are you doing here?" Tarpley demanded.

"What are *we* doing here?" Frank echoed. "We

can ask you the same thing." Frank saw that Tarpley was holding a tire iron.

"All I've got to do is pick up the phone, and you clowns will be arrested for breaking and entering," Tarpley said, tapping the tire iron against the palm of his hand.

"And you think the police will give you a medal?" Joe said. "Don't you think they might wonder what you were doing, going through closets and desks?"

Frank moved a step to one side.

"No, you don't!" Tarpley snapped at him. "Nobody's going anywhere."

Joe braced himself for action as Tarpley charged at Frank. Caught between the file cabinet and Tarpley, Frank was trapped. Joe looked on in horror as Tarpley raised the tire iron high over his shoulder, then started to swing.

Frank bobbed, but the tire iron hit him on the shoulder. Frank gasped in pain, staggered, then started to slump to the floor.

As Tarpley raised the tire iron over his shoulder again, Joe lunged across the room in a flying tackle. He hit Tarpley in the legs, and they both crashed to the floor. But before he did, Tarpley threw the tire iron directly at Frank's head.

Tarpley was quick, but Joe knew that his brother was quicker and would be able to judge Tarpley's throw to a fraction of an inch.

Frank sprang backward, neatly sidestepping the

attack. The lethal tire iron missed him by at least a foot.

Tarpley struggled to free himself from Joe's grasp, but the younger Hardy now had the man pinned in a full nelson hold.

"Good work," Frank said, grinning at his brother. He looked down at Tarpley. "The police will want to question you about the kidnapping and assault of Callie Shaw."

"Yeah, right," Tarpley said with a scowl. "You can't prove anything."

"Get up," Joe said, releasing the mechanic, who got to his feet.

"I'm outta here," Tarpley said, starting for the door.

Frank blocked the office door. "The only place you're going is prison," he said in a determined tone.

Tarpley sneered. "What is this? A citizen's arrest?"

"Joe," Frank said, "call Detective Riley."

"Don't be hasty now," Tarpley said, reaching for the phone. "I just don't like people messing in my business."

"It's our business when you kidnap my girlfriend and endanger her life, or when someone runs us off the road," Frank said, hoping Tarpley would confess that he was responsible for the incidents. "And Joe could have been killed in that warehouse when the shelves were pushed onto him."

115

"I did that stuff just to scare you off," Tarpley insisted. "Nobody got hurt. And I was just told to send a few warnings, that's all."

"Who are you working with?" Joe asked. "Curt Kiser or Jason Dain—or someone else?"

Tarpley stared sullenly at the floor.

"What were you doing at Miyagi Motors yesterday?" Frank demanded. "Were you offering to sell them the stolen circuitry diagrams to the PEST system?"

Frank watched Tarpley closely. The man's eyes widened in alarm. "I'm not talking," Tarpley growled.

"You want to go to prison for the entire scheme?" Frank asked.

"Why did you steal the Saurion?" Joe asked.

"You'll find out," Tarpley snapped. "But you aren't sending me to any prison." With a suddenness that caught Frank and Joe off-guard, Tarpley grabbed a swivel chair and threw it into Frank's legs. Frank fell forward onto the chair, and Tarpley then shoved the chair and Frank away. Seeing that the path to the door was free, Tarpley bolted out of the office and down the hallway.

"Hurry!" Frank cried, rushing out the door. "Tarpley's getting away!"

13 The Missing Driver

Frank pulled open the glass door that led outside the building and ran down the steps. Joe was right behind him.

"There he is!" Frank exclaimed, pointing to Tarpley, who was running toward a white panel truck parked in the lot.

"Someone else is in the truck, too," Joe called.

Marvin Tarpley jumped behind the wheel of the truck. He had the engine started in seconds. In the lead, Frank sprinted across the parking area. Tarpley accelerated, and dust and gravel flew up from the truck's drive wheels.

"The front gate's closed," Joe called as he caught up with his brother. "He's trapped."

When Tarpley didn't slow down and didn't even

117

hit the brakes, Joe expected a collision. Instead, the gate swung open on its own.

"The gate's on remote control," Frank said as the truck bounced out onto the road. "That explains how he got in here in the first place," Frank added as the gate swung closed. "He'll be long gone by the time we get to the Saurion."

"I think I know who the other person in Dain's office was," Joe said. He pulled the piece of material out of his pocket.

"It's a red silk scarf," Frank said. "Katie Bratton's scarf."

Joe nodded. "That was probably Katie in the truck with Tarpley."

"That means Felix Stock's trusted driver is plotting against him," Frank said.

"Then we can't let Katie drive in the race," Joe said.

"Maybe she never had any intention of driving," Frank said thoughtfully, "if she's been sabotaging the car. In any case, we've got to warn Stock, and when the office opens, we need to talk to Curt Kiser and Jason Dain. I'd be very surprised if Tarpley is the brains behind this plot. Knowing what we do now, it could be Katie Bratton."

"She did lie to us about Takeo Ota not wanting the race," Joe said. Pointing to the speedway golf cart in the lot beside the office, he added, "Since it's so far around the track, let's borrow the golf cart."

"Good idea," Frank said. "We can return the Saurion when the gate opens."

Using the track as a shortcut, Frank accelerated onto the straightaway. He drove the cart up to Building A and braked to a stop outside the open overhead door. A distraught-looking Felix Stock hurried outside to meet the Hardys.

"Have you seen Katie?" Stock asked. "I think something's happened to her. She was supposed to meet me here over an hour ago."

"When was the last time you talked to Katie?" Frank asked Stock.

"Last night," the engineer told him. "She helped me with the prototype until maybe midnight. Then she went home to get some rest. But she said she'd be here around six."

"Where *is* home?" Joe wanted to know.

"She's got an apartment on Mowrye Street. Her number is in the file in my office."

While Joe headed for Stock's office to put through a call to Katie Bratton's apartment, Frank pumped Stock for information.

"What does Katie stand to make if she wins this race?" Frank asked.

"I promised she'd receive a share of the Saurion's profits," Stock replied.

"Did you and Katie talk about any specific amount?" Frank asked.

"Not really," Stock said. "The truth is, I had a crush on Katie. When we started working togeth-

119

er on the Saurion, I hoped things might work out."

"You've changed your mind?" Frank asked.

Stock sighed deeply. "When I told Katie how I felt about her, she said she had a lot of years of auto racing ahead of her before she could give any thought to settling down."

"But she still didn't ask for a contract?" Frank asked.

"Come to think of it, she brought it up a couple of times," Stock admitted. "I told her we'd have my lawyer work something out."

"But you said you and Kiser have a contract," Frank said. "Could I see it?"

"If I can find it," Stock said, leading him into his small, cluttered office. He started rummaging around through the papers on his messy desk. "It's not here," he said finally. "I'll have to get it for you later. I've got too much to do right now."

"Katie doesn't answer," Joe announced. He hung up the phone.

"I'm sorry, Mr. Stock," Frank said gently, "but Joe and I don't think Katie Bratton ever planned to drive the Saurion today. We think she's in cahoots with Marvin Tarpley."

Felix Stock sat down dejectedly in his battered office chair. "What are you talking about?" he asked, a blank expression on his face.

Joe picked up the story. "Tarpley was snooping

around Jason Dain's office earlier this morning, and we think Katie was with him."

"Do you have any idea what she might have been looking for in Dain's office?" Frank asked.

Felix Stock frowned. "No, not at all. I trust Katie, though."

"I think we'd better call Con Riley," Frank said, reaching for the phone.

"I can't believe Marvin Tarpley would betray me, either," Stock said angrily, slamming his fist on the desk.

Frank reached Con Riley at his home. Frank told Con about Marvin Tarpley's assault on Joe and gave him descriptions of Tarpley and Bratton. "We'll file charges against Tarpley as soon as we have time," Frank told Con. "In the meantime, we need some information on brand-new white panel trucks sold in this area."

Frank waited while Con used his personal computer workstation to locate the information. Then Frank thanked the lieutenant and hung up the phone.

"From your expression," Joe said, "I'd say you got something."

Frank nodded. "I sure did. Con told me Miyagi Motors bought ten of the trucks, and one other was sold to a company called International Land and Resources. And guess who owns the company."

"Who?" Joe asked.

121

"Jason Dain," Frank announced. "And Con said those fingerprints we faxed yesterday—from the letter that was supposedly from Callie—belong to Tarpley. His prints are on file with the army."

"It looks as though you guys are getting to the bottom of this case," Stock said, still looking a little stunned. "Although I can't figure out why they wouldn't want the Saurion to win. But if they want me out of the race, they're winning. I can't drive the Saurion if Katie doesn't."

"I can," Joe said seriously. "I've already had a little experience with it at high speeds."

"Joe can do it," Frank said confidently.

"If you're willing to try it," Felix Stock said, brightening, "we won't have to forfeit. Do you know anything about tuning cars?"

"I've changed a few plugs," Joe said.

Felix Stock rubbed his hands together. "Then help me finish getting the Saurion ready," he said, breaking out into a large smile. "Maybe we can win this race yet!"

"While you two are doing that," Frank said, "I'll talk to Curt Kiser."

Frank headed the golf cart to the main office and returned the vehicle to its shed. Curt Kiser was checking a ledger in the receptionist's area when Frank walked in.

"Could we talk in private?" Frank asked Kiser.

"Sure," Kiser said. "Come on back to my office."

Kiser offered Frank a chair, then sat down at his desk.

"This is a pretty big day for the speedway, I suppose," Frank said casually.

"As a matter of fact, this *is* a big day," Kiser replied, "and I certainly don't have much time—"

"Is Jason Dain here yet?" Frank interrupted.

"No," Kiser said. "He told me yesterday he might be a little late this morning."

"On such an important day?" Frank asked, raising his eyebrows.

"Look," Kiser said, "I don't have—"

"Do you race remote-control cars?" Frank placed the power card from Building C on Kiser's blotter.

Kiser glanced at the relay and raised his eyebrows in surprise. "Yes," he said finally, "as a matter of fact, I do race remote-control cars."

"Is that power card yours?" Frank asked. "When Chet Morton showed this to you the other day, you said you didn't know what it was."

"All I meant," Kiser said slowly, "was that I've never used this brand. It's imported. Very expensive."

"How about your associate, Jason Dain?" Frank continued. "Does he race model cars?"

Curt Kiser laughed. "Dain doesn't have any hobbies. The Saurion's been found. Why do you need all this information?"

Frank ignored his question. "There's a mechanic

named Marvin Tarpley working here at the speedway. Do you know him?"

Kiser shook his head. "There are a lot of people working here that I don't know personally."

Frank changed the subject. "Did you know that Katie Bratton didn't show up this morning? We have reason to believe she won't be driving in the race."

"Who's going to drive the Saurion?" Kiser cried. "If we have to cancel that race, I'll be ruined!"

Frank watched Kiser closely. "Is there anyone who would gain from canceling this race?"

"Not me," Kiser said emphatically. "The truth is, the speedway's almost bankrupt. That's why I had to bring in the demolition derby and why we're having this sports car race."

Kiser sighed. "Anyway, I found an investor— Jason Dain. You don't think Dain is behind Stock's problems, do you?" Kiser asked. Then he shook his head. "That doesn't make sense. Why would he want to do that? This race brings in big bucks. If the track makes money, Dain makes money."

"I think the answer is in the contract you drew up with Felix Stock," Frank suggested.

Curt Kiser hesitated, then said, "I'll have my secretary make you a copy." He pressed the button in his intercom. "Stephanie," he said, "would you please make a copy of the Stock-Saurion contract for Frank Hardy? Thanks."

124

As Kiser hung up the phone, the office door opened.

"Frank Hardy?" the receptionist asked. "There's a call for you. Line two."

Kiser handed Frank the receiver, and he said hello.

"This is Taylor, mechanic over at the Saurion shop," said a hoarse voice. "Your brother's been in a bad accident."

"Is he all right?" Frank asked, alarmed.

"You better get over here," the man said.

"There's an emergency," Frank said quickly to Kiser. He bolted out of the office toward the lobby. Taking the contract from Kiser's secretary, Frank dashed past the surprised woman and out the door.

Rushing down the office's front steps, Frank was startled when he looked up and saw his own face reflected in the visor of a very short, helmeted man.

At the same moment he felt something hard jam into his ribs.

"Into the back of the truck," the man in the helmet said in a low, menacing voice.

One of the two back doors on the white panel truck stood open. Prodded by what he was sure was the barrel of a gun, Frank moved toward the truck.

The man pushed Frank roughly into the back of the truck. As Frank stumbled inside, he felt a sharp blow to the back of his head. Then everything went black.

14 Up Against the Wall

Joe, at work under the Saurion's hood, yelled across Building A to Felix Stock, "Fuel line looks good."

"And so does that racing suit. It matches the Saurion," Callie Shaw said as she entered the garage with Chet.

Chet turned to Felix Stock. "Mr. Stock, Callie parked your sedan out front. Right beside my jeep."

Joe straightened up and smiled at Callie. Then he stretched out his arms to show off the red flame-retardant suit. It had blue stripes up the side.

"This suit's made from Kevlar," Joe explained, "the same material they use for bulletproof vests."

"The driver who's going to race the Saurion ought to be wearing that outfit," Callie pointed out.

"I *am* the driver," Joe told her. He explained briefly what had happened since he and Frank had been with Chet and Callie last night.

"Where's Frank?" Callie asked.

"He had some investigating to do," Joe said. He checked his watch and frowned. "But he's been gone most of the morning."

Just then a white panel truck pulled up in front of the building. The passenger door slid back, and Takeo Ota stepped out. Joe checked out the truck's license and saw it was a temporary tag.

"Felix," Takeo Ota said warmly as he entered the building. "I want to wish you the best of luck in the race."

"Thank you, Takeo," Stock replied.

"Is your car ready to go?" Ota asked, giving the Saurion an admiring once-over.

"I've had to make one change," Stock told him. "Joe Hardy here is going to drive."

"*What?*" Takeo Ota said, looking surprised. "This is very disappointing. I was hoping for a good race." Quickly he looked at Joe. "Please don't be offended," he added. "I only meant—"

"That's okay," Joe said. "I know you were expecting Katie Bratton to drive the Saurion. But I'll give your Speedster all it can handle. By the way," he added, "I'm curious about something. Do any of your trucks have regular license plates?"

"Not yet," Mr. Ota replied. "That's why the

numbers weren't listed in the computer. The plates came in the mail this morning. And so did this." He handed Stock a manila envelope. "These belong to you."

Joe saw Stock's eyes grow wide as he pulled three sheets of paper out of the envelope. "These are my stolen wiring diagrams!" he exclaimed.

"A man tried to sell them to us," Takeo Ota explained. "As a matter of fact, he fits the description Joe and Frank gave us the other day of a person they were looking for. I told the man no, but he's still pestering me. I have already made contact with the police."

Joe asked Takeo what the man looked like, and he described someone who Joe was sure was Tarpley.

"Thank you, Takeo," Felix Stock said, shaking hands with Mr. Ota again.

The Miyagi Motors' project engineer turned and walked to the truck. "May the fastest car win," he said as he drove off.

Stepping over to Felix, Joe said, "It looks as if Tarpley's got another count against him."

"Yeah," Stock said. "Tarpley better not show his face on these grounds ever again. I wonder where he's hiding himself. Anyway, it's time to take the Saurion to the pits," Stock said, looking at the clock on the garage wall. "It'll be two o'clock soon."

Joe grabbed a red and blue striped racing helmet

and a pair of driving gloves. "I'm sure Frank will track down Tarpley sooner or later," he said.

"Where am I?" Frank Hardy asked himself. His head ached, and he felt a knot just above his neck.

At first he thought he had been blindfolded, but then he realized he was back in one of the underground utility tunnels. He also realized that the person who knocked him out wasn't Marvin Tarpley. The person had been very short, barely five feet tall. Frank was sure it was Katie Bratton.

He sat up very slowly, not wanting to draw attention to himself if someone was guarding him. He listened carefully for a minute, then decided he was alone. Frank crawled across the floor until he reached a wall. Fighting the feeling of dizziness, he braced himself against the tunnel's side. He checked to see if Kiser's contract was still stuffed in his back pocket. It was.

Taking a step forward, he bumped into a table, knocking it to the concrete floor. A clatter that sounded like aluminum pie pans and the thunk of heavy metal echoed through the tunnel. He knelt down and felt along the floor. His hands touched several light metal rectangles with raised letters and numbers on them.

"That clattering sound was a stack of fake license plates," Frank murmured. He continued to feel around. Suddenly he touched a heavy steel device.

129

"And this has got to be a stamping machine. I have to get out of here and tell Joe."

Joe Hardy felt butterflies in his stomach as he looked at the cheering crowd in the speedway grandstand. He could see that every seat was taken, and hundreds of spectators stood outside the tall fence.

"This crowd is definitely ready for a race," Curt Kiser called as he passed by the pits in a brightly stickered pace car.

"And so am I!" Joe called out. Then he turned to Chet. "Something's happened to Frank," Joe said. "We didn't have any specific plans to meet, but I'm positive he wanted to be here for the start of the race. Would you look around for him?"

"Right," Chet said, taking off.

Waving to the pit crew, Joe climbed into the red Saurion and snapped on his seat belt. Bright flashes lit up the car's interior as the press photographers crowded around.

"Testing one, two, three," Callie said, walking up to the Saurion with Felix Stock. She was wearing a radio headset that allowed her to speak with Joe during the race. "Am I coming through clearly?"

"Sounds good," Joe said, and pushed the button on the remote to start the Saurion. The engine caught immediately and roared to life. Felix gave Joe the thumbs-up sign, and Joe returned it.

Joe saw a streak of yellow pass the pits. It was the

Sata Speedster, already out on the track. Joe shifted the Saurion into first and roared out onto the straightaway.

Joe saw the Sata Speedster hugging the pace car. It was weaving to heat up its tires. Joe kept his eye on the starting official as the three cars cruised around the fourth turn. Because the rules called for a flying start, Joe had to stay abreast of the Speedster until the starter dropped the green flag. Then it was one hundred laps to the victory lane.

"Go!" Callie shouted in Joe's headset when the starter dropped the green flag.

Like a rocket, the Saurion zoomed low and ahead of the Speedster. Joe's strategy was to head for the inside. The power excited him. Faintly above the roar of his car, Joe could hear the cheering of the crowd. I'm going to win this, he thought.

From the tunnel underground Frank heard the noise as the race began. "I hope Stock got those handling problems repaired," he said to himself.

Suddenly a piece of the puzzle fell into place. "Handling problems!" he exclaimed, his voice echoing in the tunnel. "It's so obvious, why didn't we think of it earlier?"

Realizing his brother was in deadly danger, Frank stepped cautiously through the tunnel, hoping to find a way out. He had walked a few yards when he saw a small beam of light shining down. He looked up and spotted a manhole cover that was partly open. He looked around and saw two rusty milk crates against the wall. He placed the crates on top of each other under the manhole cover and stepped up onto them.

Frank raised his arms and jumped. After three tries, he finally managed to push the manhole cover aside. He jumped again and grabbed the opening's lip. Slowly Frank started to pull himself up. He crawled up onto the grass and saw he was between two buildings.

As he tried to get his bearings, Chet came running up. He'd been driving his jeep around the grounds in search of Frank. "I've been looking everywhere for you!" Chet cried out. "Are you all right?"

"Is Joe driving the Saurion?" Frank asked anxiously, ignoring Chet's question.

"He sure is," Chet said, "and he's winning."

"The car's been tampered with," Frank said. "If we don't get him off that track, something terrible's going to happen."

Frank quickly climbed into the jeep beside Chet. "Hurry!" he urged.

"Callie's on the radio phone," Chet told Frank as he pointed the jeep in the direction of the pit area. "She can call him in."

Joe was beginning to think that Indy-style racing really wasn't as exciting as driving in a demolition derby. He kept the pedal to the floor and eased

132

through the turns. The onboard computer told him he was averaging 154.26 miles per hour. Not bad, he thought. Callie had told him he was well ahead of the Speedster.

Suddenly Joe sensed something was wrong. The car roared out of turn three and approached turn four too high and too close to the wall. Joe tried to bring the Saurion back, but the machine wasn't responding. He took his foot off the accelerator. The speed continued to climb, from 162 miles per hour to 164.

"Frank!" Callie cried as he and Chet jolted to a stop behind the pit area. "Joe said he can't control the Saurion." Callie removed the headphones. She'd been relaying all of Joe's messages to Felix. She handed Frank the earphones.

Frank had to shout above the crowd into the earphones. "Joe, you're going to lose control. Back off a bit."

"Can't," Joe said curtly. "The pedals don't work, and neither does the steering."

Frank told his brother to hang on. "I don't have time to explain," he added, giving the earphones back to Callie, "but the car's been rigged. Katie Bratton, Tarpley, maybe even Jason Dain—one of them is driving the Saurion by remote control, and they don't intend for Joe to win. Or even finish."

"What are you talking about?" Felix Stock asked.

"They installed remote-control devices in your

133

car," Frank explained hurriedly. "The electronics override the steering, accelerator, and brakes. Someone even rigged the silver Saurion so the PEST system would go black last night."

Spotting Curt Kiser not far away, Frank ran over to the speedway owner. "Where's Jason Dain?" he asked.

"Dain? He should be up in the tower."

Frank turned and looked up at the officials' tower. He didn't see Dain.

"You mean the Saurion's being operated like one of Curt Kiser's remote-control cars?" Stock asked when Frank returned.

"Exactly," Frank said. "When we found the Saurion down in the tunnel, there were marks on the inside of the brake disks. One of those crooks installed receivers and solenoids there and in other spots. Now we've got to find the person who has the control box."

"Frank!" Callie cried suddenly. "Look at the Saurion!"

Frank could see his brother fighting for control of the sports car. Joe was whizzing by at speeds well beyond the red line.

"He's doing one ninety!" Stock read from his stopwatch.

"He's going to beat the Speedster," Chet said.

"With the course he's on now," Frank said, "Joe's going to *hit* the Speedster."

"Joe," Callie called into the headset several

times. "I can't talk to him," she said to Frank. "All of a sudden I'm getting static."

Joe turned off the squawking radio and said to himself, "I don't know who's driving this car, but it sure isn't me."

Suddenly it dawned on him. The Saurion was being guided by remote control. "That's what happened when I test drove the Saurion the other day, and that's why the Saurion was stolen," he said aloud, "so they could install the power cards and the solenoids that would operate the brakes, accelerator, and steering."

Not needing to steer, Joe examined the cockpit closely. The solenoids would be attached to the wheels, or steering gears, but Joe knew the devices required antennas.

"That's it!" he cried out triumphantly. Reaching up to the windshield frame, he felt a thin wire without insulation. Pulling it loose, he discovered it went down the side post and under the dashboard. Tracing it beneath the dashboard, Joe gripped it firmly and pulled. The wire snapped. At the same time the car veered suddenly toward the outside wall. Joe grabbed the steering wheel, bringing the Saurion back under control. He caught up with the Speedster and whizzed past, missing it by inches.

Joe saw by the speedometer that he was doing 190. "That wire only controlled the steering," he said to himself. And now that he had to steer again, he couldn't search further in the cockpit.

Meanwhile, Frank took charge in the pits. "We've got to find Jason Dain and Katie Bratton. Callie, stay on the phone in case Joe comes back on. Chet and I will look for Dain and Bratton."

Frank leapt over the pit wall and headed for the tower. He took the steep wooden stairs two at a time. "Stay close," he instructed Chet.

Reaching the top, he quickly scanned the group of racing officials.

"Is Jason Dain here?" Frank asked.

"Over in the press box," a man answered.

Frank and Chet scrambled back down the stairs, then headed for the concrete underpass that ran beneath the track. Leading the way, Frank bolted up the aisle toward the press box at the top of the grandstand.

Slipping quickly through the press box door, Frank made his way behind the officials to a door beyond that led into the owner's box.

Suddenly the door burst open, and Jason Dain bolted out.

"What's going on here?" a speedway security guard demanded.

"This man is a suspect in a case involving assault, fraud, and attempted murder," Frank told the guard. "Chet, call Con Riley."

"Go ahead!" Dain spat out. "It's only a few minutes before the bomb in the Saurion explodes." Then Dain feinted right, trying to fake his way past Frank.

Frank was quick to react. He chopped Dain first in the stomach, then hit him square on the chin. Jason Dain dropped like a rock.

Frank frisked Dain, but he did not have the remote control.

"He said there's a bomb," Chet said in a frightened voice.

"I heard him," Frank said grimly. "There's no time to lose. We've got to save Joe!"

15 The Winner's Circle

Frank knew Katie Bratton was the one to find. But where was she?

Impatiently he scanned the speedway grounds. Frustration gripped him as he realized the crowd was in the hundreds. His eyes rested on a white panel truck parked in front of the demolition derby's main garage. The area around the truck was empty.

Out of the corner of his eye, Frank glimpsed something move on the roof of a garage. He looked over and saw two figures on the roof. "Chet, let's go," Frank said. Frank and Chet dashed downstairs.

Callie waved and caught up to them. "Stock's on the radio, talking to Joe," she said.

"I've spotted Katie Bratton," Frank said, pointing back toward the infield from which Callie had just come.

Frank, Callie, and Chet headed through the service tunnel that passed under the middle of the main straightaway.

Frank exited the tunnel and dashed toward the derby garage. Callie and Chet were right behind him. Chet gave him a boost, and Frank pulled himself quietly up the spouting to the roof.

Looking over, Frank could see Katie and Tarpley. Katie had the remote-control device in her hand. Marvin was leaning over the low cement-block wall that ringed the roof.

"You got him running every which way but backward," Tarpley said.

Katie laughed gleefully. "When I activate the relays connected to the fuel injection, the Saurion will just keep picking up speed. Even I couldn't control a car under those circumstances."

"You're a genius," Tarpley said admiringly.

Frank lunged across the tar-paper roof toward Katie. In one smooth motion he turned Katie around and grabbed the remote control from her hands.

"Hey!" Tarpley protested. But before he could make a move, Frank turned and smashed him in the jaw. Tarpley slumped limply to the roof.

Katie Bratton recovered quickly enough to snatch

the remote back. Frank stumbled as he reached out to stop her. Then, just as it looked as though Katie might get away, Callie appeared at the edge of the roof.

"Got her!" Callie called to Frank as she grabbed one of Katie's legs. Frank hurried over to the struggling girls. Katie was holding the deadly remote control close to her body.

"Get your hands off me!" Katie screamed. She had the remote in her right hand. Callie gripped her right wrist. Katie was trying to press a small red button in the remote's upper left corner.

"Drop it!" Frank ordered Katie as he grabbed her right hand and twisted her wrist. Suddenly she lashed out with her foot, kicking Callie in the side. Out of breath, Callie loosened her grip.

Finally Frank managed to rip the remote out of Katie's hand. It clattered across the garage. Frank ran over to the remote, but not in time to stop Tarpley from snatching it up.

"So much for Joe Hardy and the Saurion!" Tarpley sneered as he straightened the antenna and checked the power switch.

Before Frank could reach the mechanic, Tarpley had pushed the red button.

Frank tensed as he waited for the sound of the bomb to go off. When nothing happened, he lunged at the mechanic, forcing Tarpley backward.

Frank and Tarpley tumbled over the edge of the

roof. Frank heard Tarpley cry out. Frank felt himself falling. Then, as he hit something firm but rubbery, he heard a familiar voice.

"Put your hands up, Tarpley," Detective Con Riley ordered. Then Riley searched Tarpley.

"Good thing you landed on that pile of old tires," Chet said as he helped Frank to his feet.

"Callie's still up on the roof with Katie Bratton," Frank said breathlessly.

He looked up and saw Callie. She was holding both of Katie Bratton's arms behind her back. The driver was standing quietly, her head down and her blond hair falling over her face.

"No problem," Callie called down to them. "I've got things under control here."

Frank helped Callie and Katie Bratton get down from the roof, and then watched Con Riley put the cuffs on Katie.

"I didn't do anything!" Katie Bratton insisted sullenly. "It was all Marvin's idea."

"She planned the whole thing," Tarpley blurted out. "She and Jason Dain."

Katie's eyes flashed. "Shut up, you fool!"

"I know you were making counterfeit license plates for the white panel truck," Frank said. "I found the stamping machine in the tunnel this afternoon."

"That was Dain," Tarpley insisted. "He wanted you to think Miyagi Motors was doing everything."

"It wasn't Dain who left us to die in that tunnel fire," Frank said. "That was you, Tarpley."

"Hey, a guy's got to look out for himself," Tarpley insisted. A look of satisfaction came over his face.

"How did you get out of the warehouse after pushing the shelves on Joe?" Frank asked.

Tarpley laughed. "While you were looking at the skylights, I was slipping down a manhole into the tunnels. You never even knew where to look." Shrugging, Tarpley said, "If the Saurion burns in a tunnel or wrecks on the track, what's the difference? When that bomb goes off, Joe Hardy's dead meat."

"It's too late for that, Tarpley," Callie reminded him. "You pushed the red button and nothing happened."

"That's because all the red button does is set the timer," he said smugly.

Frank grabbed Tarpley's shirt. "Where is that timer?"

"Shut up, Marvin!" Katie Bratton ordered.

While Con Riley locked the cuffs on Tarpley, Frank said again, "Where is it?"

"The device is wired to the brakes," Tarpley admitted. "It's set to detonate at exactly seventy-seven minutes into the race." Tarpley paused, then sneered. "If your brother doesn't stop the Saurion, he's going to have to set a speed record to get out of it alive."

142

Callie and Chet hurried after Frank to the pit area. The infield sign indicated that two laps remained in the race.

Felix Stock's eyes were glued to the speeding cars. "Joe's ahead of the Speedster," he told Frank.

"We've got to wave Joe in," Frank said. "There's a bomb wired to the brakes."

"A bomb!" Felix Stock exclaimed. His face was frozen in shock.

"How many minutes into the race is he?" Frank demanded.

Stock checked his stop watch. "About seventy-five minutes, ten seconds," he replied. "With just under two laps to go."

"Give me the radio," Frank said.

"The radio's acting up. We'll have to use a sign."

Joe had found all of a sudden that the accelerator and brakes were controllable. He figured that his brother had found and stopped whoever was operating the remote. He could also see in his mirror that the Sata Speedster was trying to catch up with him. There was only one and a half laps to go.

In spite of the danger Joe wanted to win. He pressed down on the accelerator and cut diagonally toward the white line along the infield.

"Pull in!" Frank shouted as he held up the sign reading "Pit Now!"

Joe ignored it. The Saurion roared past the pit area into its final lap, its needle edging past two

143

hundred. The crowd was on its feet, roaring its approval of the hard-run race.

Frank saw that the Speedster's driver was doing a great job. He couldn't be more than a couple seconds behind.

"Hold on, baby!" Joe urged the machine. Suddenly Joe heard static in his headset, then Frank's voice. "Joe! Can you hear me? There's a . . ." Then static broke up the signal.

"Cross your fingers!" Joe shouted into the headset. "I'm coming in for the finish."

"Expl . . . set to—" Joe heard Frank say.

Joe saw the yellow Speedster was pulling out to pass.

Could he make it to the finish line first? "I've got to try," Joe told himself. He knew he could make the car go faster. He downshifted to fourth and eased out the clutch. Joe felt himself forced back into the seat as the Saurion leapt ahead.

Joe widened the gap between his car and the Speedster, and as the two cars sped around the fourth turn into the straightaway, Joe held the shifter in fifth and pressed the accelerator full out.

Ahead, Joe could see the checkered flag. "Just a few more yards," he said to himself.

"He's done it!" Felix Stock yelled as the Saurion crossed the finish line a car length ahead of the Speedster. "And he set a track record."

Suddenly a blinding flash erupted from the

Saurion's front wheel well. Frank held his breath as the sports car swerved and made a hard left toward the infield. The Speedster steered nimbly around the stricken Saurion.

Joe felt the steering go the moment the bomb exploded. He also caught sight of his left front wheel assembly flying up into the air. The front end dropped, and a shower of sparks sprayed up as the shattered suspension arms screeched across the pavement.

Fortunately, the force of the bomb blew outward, away from the engine. The powerful V-8 was still running, but Joe found that the front brakes had been destroyed in the explosion. He tried slowing the car the same way he had the first time he'd driven it. He shifted into reverse.

The car slowed so dramatically, it slammed against the side wall at the end of the straightaway. Joe felt himself thrown forward and sideways against the safety belt. He had totally lost control of the Saurion, but at least the car was slowing down.

The car rebounded off the wall, then slid to a stop in the middle of the track. Joe slipped out of his racing harness and stepped out of the smoking car.

A mechanic hurried over with a fire extinguisher and began to douse the flames.

Frank rushed up to Joe. "Are you okay?" Frank asked anxiously.

"That was some wild ride," Chet said.

"You could have told me there was a bomb in the car," Joe commented dryly. "Other than that," he added with a grin, "it was a piece of cake."

"You won!" Felix Stock exclaimed as Joe, Frank, and Chet returned to the pit area. Stock began pumping Joe's hand.

"I dropped another transmission," Joe admitted.

"I've come to expect it," Felix Stock said, chuckling. "It's still a great beginning for my Saurion."

Frank turned to Felix Stock. "I read your contract while Chet drove me to the pits," he told the designer. "The mystery's solution was right there. Katie Bratton and Jason Dain were plotting to get control of the Saurion, particularly your PEST patent."

"The contract would allow that?" Stock asked.

Frank nodded. "Should the Saurion fail or otherwise prove itself unprofitable within one year, everything connected with the car becomes the property of the speedway.

"But Curt Kiser owns the speedway," Felix Stock said, looking with surprise at Kiser, who had just joined them.

"Not exactly," Curt Kiser said with a sigh. "To get Dain to back me, I had to give him exclusive rights to any property acquired by the speedway."

"Unfortunately," Frank explained, "that meant the Saurion. The prototype could be destroyed, but there were the other cars you had been working on. Dain figured the Saurion would be a dead car after

146

the destruction of the prototype. Then Dain planned to use your design and PEST system to create his own sports car and make a fortune. Tarpley was trying to make his own fortune by offering the wiring diagrams to Miyagi Motors."

Kiser sighed. "I'm sorry, Felix. I never intended it to turn out that way."

"Dain, Tarpley, and Bratton are on their way to police headquarters," Con Riley told the group as he entered the pit area. "And you'll be happy to know they were blaming each other for the threats and sabotage. It seems that Katie and Jason were originally responsible for the scheme. Then Tarpley found out, but they didn't want to cut him in, so Katie said the deal was off."

"That's probably why we heard Tarpley in the diner threatening Katie's life if she drove the car," Frank said.

"Tarpley had the wiring plans," Riley continued, "which he used to blackmail Dain and Bratton."

"So if they excluded him from their plans," Joe said, "they couldn't stop him from trying to sell the wiring diagrams because he could have exposed them."

"Tarpley also threatened Katie with a note," Riley said, "but Jason Dain admitted he was the one who phoned Felix with the threat about the death car."

"I guess Katie showed us the note so we wouldn't consider her a suspect," Frank said.

"That's right," Riley said. "Tarpley admitted to planting the stereo in Chet's jeep, and Dain admitted installing a remote dimmer device on the new Saurion. Tarpley was following last night in a white panel truck with the control that made the windows darken."

"That truck was part of the scheme," Frank said. "Dain bought it because he knew Miyagi Motors had purchased ten of them. By driving the same kind of vehicle, he thought it might throw suspicion on the Speedster's owners."

"Did I hear someone mention the Sata Speedster?" Takeo Ota asked as he stepped into the Saurion's pit from the Speedster's. He shook hands warmly with Felix Stock. "Congratulations," he said.

"Thanks," Stock said. "But it was Joe Hardy who did the work."

Before he left the pit, Mr. Ota said, "Good luck with your Saurion, Felix."

"And with your Speedster, Takeo," Stock told him, smiling. Then he sighed. "I should have paid closer attention to my business," he said.

"That makes two of us," Curt Kiser admitted.

"We'd better get down to the police station with Detective Riley to file our reports," Frank said.

"That reminds me," Con Riley said. "I've already seen to it that all charges against Chet Morton were dropped."

Chet smiled broadly.

148

"There is one thing, though," the detective continued, grinning at Chet. "When we were searching for that stereo, we saw that your jeep looked pretty beat-up. Before we can permit you to drive it, you need to have it inspected. That thing looks like it's been through a demolition derby." The group laughed and agreed.

"It'll never pass inspection, Chet. Face it," Joe said.

Chet groaned.

"Then you're going to need a loaner," Felix said. "Here's the remote to the silver Saurion."

"Wow!" Chet exclaimed, taking the remote and staring at it. "Thanks, Mr. Stock."

"Be careful with it, though," Joe said with a grin. "The transmissions on those cars are really temperamental."

THE HARDY BOYS® SERIES By Franklin W. Dixon

AND DON'T FORGET...NANCY DREW CASEFILES® AVAILABLE FROM PAPERBACK